IGOR™

MOVIE NOVELIZATION

In life, you are either a somebody or a nobody. And here in Malaria, the biggest somebodies are Evil Scientists.

—Igor

This book is a work of fiction. Any references to historical events, real people, or real locales are used fictitiously. Other names, characters, places, and incidents are the product of the author's imagination, and any resemblance to actual events or locales or persons, living or dead, is entirely coincidental.

SIMON SPOTLIGHT
An imprint of Simon & Schuster Children's Publishing Division
1230 Avenue of the Americas, New York, New York 10020
Igor © 2008 Exodus Film Fund I, LLC. All rights reserved. *Igor*™, and the names of the characters, events, items, and places therein, are trademarks of Exodus Film Fund I, LLC, under license to Simon & Schuster. All rights reserved.
All rights reserved, including the right of reproduction in whole or in part in any form.
SIMON SPOTLIGHT and colophon are registered trademarks of Simon & Schuster, Inc.
Manufactured in the United States of America
First Edition 10 9 8 7 6 5 4 3 2 1
ISBN 13: 978-1-4169-5364-7
ISBN 10: 1-4169-5364-7

MOVIE NOVELIZATION

adapted by Catherine Hapka
based on the screenplay by Chris McKenna

SIMON SPOTLIGHT
New York   London   Toronto   Sydney

ONE

It was a dark, miserable night in Malaria. It was *always* dark and miserable in Malaria.

The entire country was dismal. Angry storm clouds rumbled with constant thunder. Craggy mountains and angular stone castles cast long, jagged shadows with every sickening flash of sulfurous lightning. Most of the plants had wilted and died off long ago, leaving only stunted, twisted trees.

A portly hunchback named Igor trudged through a cemetery dragging a wooden cart. He looked up. Lightning lit up the eternal night, exposing a limp, skinny body hanging from a noose on a tree.

"What are you doing?" Igor asked.

"What does it look like I'm doing?" the body answered.

Igor sighed. "You can't die, Scamper."

Scamper was a creepy-looking rabbit with long, stringy ears and a metal cap welded to his skull. He had an eternally negative outlook.

"Yeah," Scamper said bitterly. "Thanks to you and your irritating inventions."

"You're my most irritating invention so far," Igor replied. He cut the rope and Scamper fell into his cart with a thud.

Igor trudged slowly toward home. That home was the castle of Dr. Glickenstein, one of Malaria's leading Evil Scientists.

Evil Scientists were the rock stars of Malaria. Every year the best of them competed to create the world's most diabolical weapon. Once the winner was declared, other countries paid Malaria *not* to unleash its new evil weapon on them. Malaria got rich, the Evil Scientists got fame and fortune, and life was good for all Malarians . . . unless you happened to be born with a hunch on your back. Then you were stuck with life as an Igor, merely a lowly, humble assistant to an Evil Scientist, your very life subject to his whims and tempers. In that case, your existence could be summed up in two words: "Yes, master!"

But Igor had made up his mind to change the course of his predetermined life. Later, as he pored over his latest scientific plans in his tiny room in the depths of the cold stone castle, he pondered his plight. Perhaps there was a way to escape his dreary life as a mere—

"*IGOR!*"

Igor snapped out of his daydream at the sound of Dr. Glickenstein's voice. The impatient tone of his shout made it clear that the scientist had been calling him for a while. Quickly stuffing his plans back into the thin metal canister he wore around his neck, Igor rushed for the stairs.

"Sorry, master," he panted as he burst into the scientist's lab.

Dr. Glickenstein glared at him. "What did you say?"

Igor gulped, realizing his mistake: He had answered in his normal voice! "I mean . . ." He switched to the slurred, dull-sounding voice that all Igors used in front of their masters. "Sorry, master. I was in the bathroom. Had a bat stuck in the belfry, if you know what I mean."

Dr. Glickenstein was annoyed. He rubbed his left hand with his specially designed robotic right one. He had lost his original right hand in an unfortunate lab accident.

"I give you five minutes a week to take care of your business," the Evil Scientist snapped. "I'm not running a resort here, you know!"

"Yes, master," Igor replied.

"Now, if we're done with your toilet memoirs . . ." the

scientist said, before barking out, "Pull the switch!"

"Yes, master." Igor hurried over to a switch on the wall. He threw it, and electricity began to surge through the lab. Dr. Glickenstein's latest evil invention started humming under its protective sheet, and the scientist smiled—until a sudden burst of sparks and sizzles crackled from under the sheet. The invention shuddered . . . before coming to a complete stop.

The Evil Scientist screamed in frustration. "I should have become a travel agent like my mother said!" he cried. "I was never meant to be a scientist." He pointed to Igor. "You! Go find me a sixteen gigawatt temporal transducer."

Igor hesitated, knowing that his master was about to make a big mistake. "Excuse me, master," he slurred. "Are you sure you don't mean a *twenty-one* gigawatt?"

Dr. Glickenstein frowned. "*You're* correcting *me*?" He grabbed Igor with his robotic hand and tossed him across the lab. Igor rolled into a row of canisters, sending them flying like bowling pins. "Strike!" Dr. Glickenstein shouted with glee, then stormed out of the lab.

Igor sat up and rubbed his back. "Oww, my hunch," he moaned, before popping his hunch back into place with a loud *crack*. "Ah, much better."

He spotted Scamper nearby, holding on to the end of a chain. With his eyes, Igor followed the chain upward and saw that the other end was attached to a giant metal ball high overhead.

Igor sighed as Scamper released the ball. It plummeted down and crushed the rabbit beneath its immense weight.

A moment later Igor laid Scamper's squashed corpse on a concrete slab, then watched as it slowly expanded back to its normal shape.

Scamper sat up. "Will nothing end this vicious cycle?" he cried in frustration.

Igor had no answer for him. Neither did the other figure that appeared beside the slab. Well, not a *figure*, exactly. It was more like a brain in a jar . . . on wheels . . . with a robotic arm that had a clamp at its end.

"No fair!" the brain whined. "You wasted your Immortality Formula on the wrong guy, Igor. *I* want to live forever!"

"Really, Brain?" Scamper said wearily. "You want to be trapped in an endless nightmare, forced to keep living even though nothing matters?"

Brain looked confused. "Possibly. Uh, what did you just say?"

"Too bad Igor wasted his Intelligence Formula on me

too, Brain," Scamper said with a slight smirk. "Or should I say, *Brian*?"

He pointed to the label on Brain's jar. Scrawled on it was the name "Brian."

"Hey!" Brain protested. "I was in a hurry." He scowled as he added, "Stupid permanent marker."

Igor had just glanced up at a clock on the wall of the lab. It was the Countdown Clock, and it read: 7 DAYS UNTIL THE EVIL SCIENCE FAIR.

"Enough!" he told his two science experiments. "The Evil Science Fair is in a week, and Glickenstein is going to lose again."

"Okay, I get it," Brain said cheerfully. "You don't have to beg me, Igor. You want *me* to fix his invention. Now, I'll just need a screwdriver, some nails, and my bag of marbles. . . ."

"Don't touch his invention, Brain," Igor warned.

Brain frowned, insulted. "You're just jealous, like you were when I created that new word for good-bye." He prepared to storm off indignantly. "Well, *snarfog*, Igor! Snarfog forever!"

Igor rolled his eyes. "Do you know what he'd do to me if I fixed it? The same thing he'd do if he found out I invented you two."

He looked at a sign on the wall that said IGOR RECYCLING. It hung above the opening to a chute. There was a chute like that in every Evil Castle in Malaria.

"He'd recycle me," Igor said with a shudder. "Can you imagine being chopped up and used for body parts?" Then he frowned at the unfairness of it all. "If I had my shot, I could be one of the greatest Evil Scientists Malaria has ever seen . . . just like the great Dr. Schadenfreude!"

TWO

Meanwhile, in another castle in another part of Malaria, a broodingly handsome man was playing the piano. He finished the piece with a flourish, then turned to face his audience, who rewarded his performance with enthusiastic applause.

The pianist, Dr. Schadenfreude, was not only an accomplished musician, but the winner of the last seventeen Evil Science Fairs. If Evil Scientists were rock stars, Dr. Schadenfreude was Elvis, the king of all of them.

"Thank you, you're too kind," he told his audience. He was throwing a big black-tie party for the most important people in Malaria. "This is the land of evil, people. Act like it!"

The crowd laughed and clapped even louder. But Dr. Schadenfreude's girlfriend, Jaclyn, looked a little annoyed. She had been dutifully playing the triangle during the performance and had yet to be acknowledged.

Jaclyn tapped on her triangle over and over until Dr. Schadenfreude finally noticed. He swept a hand in her direction.

"My girlfriend, Jaclyn," he added. "She may seem like a shallow and conniving wench, but . . . well, that pretty much sums her up."

The crowd cheered. Jaclyn smiled, basking in the attention.

"He belittles because he loves," she said.

"I want to welcome all of you to my annual pre–Evil Science Fair party," Dr. Schadenfreude went on, "especially some of my rival Evil Scientists."

He looked directly at two of his guests. One was a round, puffy little man who looked like a blowfish. The other man had the head of a baby.

"Dr. Herzschlag may come in last in the Evil Science Fair, but he's first in the buffet line," Dr. Schadenfreude said, gesturing toward the bloated-looking man. Then he turned to the second man and smiled. "And Dr. Kindermann, I see you're still experimenting with that Youth Formula."

As the other guests chuckled, Dr. Herzschlag and Dr. Kindermann pretended to be amused. Meanwhile Jaclyn raised her glass.

"A toast!" she cried. "To the greatest Evil Genius in the world!"

Dr. Schadenfreude beamed, enjoying all the attention. But this warm and fuzzy moment was suddenly interrupted by a blast of horns. A Royal Guard strode into the ballroom.

"Bow for the king!" the guard commanded.

Everyone in the room did as they were told, except for Dr. Schadenfreude. The scientist scowled, annoyed by the untimely intrusion. Why did the king always have to try to steal his thunder?

King Malbert entered, wearing his customary affable smile. He strolled over to Dr. Schadenfreude.

"The greatest Evil Genius in the world," the king said to Dr. Schadenfreude. "I remember when people used to call *me* that, back when the clouds destroyed our peaceful land of farmers and my plan to blackmail the world saved us all."

Dr. Schadenfreude gritted his teeth. "Your Majesty, so glad you could attend."

The king chuckled. "My invitation must have gotten lost in the mail."

"It is an honor that you have graced us with your royal presence," the scientist replied, "whether or not you were invited."

"Ha-ha! I wouldn't miss it," the king said. "After all, the annual Evil Science Fair was *my* idea."

Dr. Schadenfreude forced a polite smile. "Yes," he agreed. "As you've told us. Over and over and over and over."

"Although I never competed, I used to be quite the little scientist," the king mused cheerfully.

"Yes, it's funny," Dr. Schadenfreude said with a frown. "I've never heard of any of your inventions."

The king smirked. "Maybe I'm just humble. Kind of like your beginnings."

As soon as he could, the scientist made an excuse and rushed out of the ballroom, with his Igor and Jaclyn right behind him. He waited until they were in his smoke-filled lab, which was equipped with all the latest and greatest high-tech equipment. Then he let his true feelings burst out.

"I wanna shove a pickle right where the sun don't shine!" Dr. Schadenfreude cried.

Dr. Schadenfreude's Igor looked confused. "'Where the sun don't shine'?" he repeated. "You mean Malaria, master?"

But the Evil Scientist didn't bother to answer his Igor's question. Instead, he threw his cocktail glass angrily at the

Igor, then turned to Jaclyn. He had had enough of King Malbert and his remarks.

"No matter how many Evil Science Fairs I win, I always have to bow down to that idiot. I'll never get the respect *he* gets!"

Jaclyn shrugged. "You just need to keep on winning."

An evil smile spread across Dr. Schadenfreude's face as he realized she was right. "But this year I won't stop at just winning the Evil Science Fair," he told her. "This year I'm going to unleash my winning invention on the king's smug little face. And then *he'll* be the one groveling at *my* feet!"

Later that day—or night, rather—Igor entered Dr. Glickenstein's lab carrying a box of transducers. The Evil Scientist was sitting at his desk studying some plans.

Suddenly someone yodeled outside. "A-dodle-dodle-day-hee-hoo!"

Igor dropped the box and stared as the scientist's beautiful, blond, pig-tailed girlfriend, Heidi, entered the lab. Igor had always had a crush on her.

But as usual Heidi ignored him, looking only at Dr. Glickenstein as she carried a tray of hot cocoa over to the desk. "Your little Heidi is here to help you in your last days of invention making," she sang.

She picked up his plans to make room for the tray, but Dr. Glickenstein snatched them away. "Wait! You'll spill on my plans," he complained as he hastily rolled them up and put them away in a drawer.

Then he noticed Igor. "My transducer!" he exclaimed, hurrying over to grab the box. He shooed Heidi out of the lab. "Time to go! I have no time for cocoa!"

When she was gone, the scientist peered into the box. "Why are there two in here?" he demanded.

Igor smiled nervously. "Master, the twenty-one gigawatts might be somewhat safer, I think."

"Think? Igors don't think!" Dr. Glickenstein yelled. "I'm using the sixteen gigawatts, you fool!" He threw the extra transducer at Igor. Then he scooted to his invention and ducked under the sheet.

Igor watched. There was a lot of grunting and moving around under the sheet for the next couple of minutes. Then the Evil Scientist finally emerged, rubbing his hands together with anticipation.

"That should do it," he said. Snapping his fingers at Igor, Dr. Glickenstein ordered, "Pull the switch!"

"Y-yes, master!" Igor had a bad feeling about this. A *very* bad feeling. But what could he do? He was just an Igor.

Zap! Once again, the invention started humming. And this time it kept on humming. Dr. Glickenstein was elated.

"Yes!" The scientist howled in triumph, yanking off the sheet. "Who's a failure now? Behold my rocket ship, born to stream through the world, unleashing pain and misery in her wake. I call her *Gladys*. I named her after you, Mother!" He laughed evilly. "Now to take my masterpiece for a test drive. . . ."

He rushed toward the door of the rocket ship. Igor gulped.

"Master, no!" he exclaimed. "It's dangerous. Please listen to me."

Glickenstein paused just long enough to glare at him. "Okay, I'll listen to you," he snapped. "I'll listen to you scream when I throw you down the Igor Recycling chute right after I get back." With that, he hopped into the rocket ship and reached for the controls.

"No, master!" Igor cried. "The rocket is going to—"

BLAM! The rocket burst into a million shards.

". . . explode," Igor finished uselessly. He could hardly believe it. The rocket ship was gone. So was Dr. Glickenstein, just like that. The only recognizable thing remaining was his robotic hand, which clattered to the floor and rolled under the desk.

THREE

Scamper and Brain popped into sight. "Finally!" Scamper said. "Now I can throw out that rug in the foyer. That thing is hideous." When Igor and Brain gave him looks, he shrugged. "We were all thinking it. I just said it."

At that moment there was a loud knock on the front door. Igor jumped. "Oh no, who's that?" he cried. "What am I going to do?"

"Relax, this is Glickenstein's castle," Scamper said coolly. "He doesn't have to open that door for anyone."

"Open for the king!" a muffled voice shouted from the other side of the door.

"Except for the king," Scamper corrected himself.

"He's here to see Glickenstein!" Igor cried. "What do I tell him?"

"Tell him the truth," Scamper said with a shrug.

"Glickenstein died in a lab accident."

"Right," Igor said, relieved. "The truth. That's a good option, right. Right, right."

Scamper and Brain scurried off to hide as Igor opened the door. King Malbert strode in, calling out cheerfully, "Glicky! Glicky, my boy!" He glanced around, then finally peered at Igor. "Where's Glicky?"

"Your Highness," Igor answered nervously, "he's . . . gone."

"Hmmph," the king snorted, clearly assuming that the Igor simply meant that his master was not around at the moment. "I need to see how his invention is coming. Schadenfreude is getting too cocky. Someone has to beat him this year. Someone with a brilliant Evil Invention!"

Igor gently touched the canister around his neck. It was a little overwhelming to have the king right there in front of him. It made him feel bold.

"Your Highness," Igor ventured, "Dr. Glickenstein is . . . is . . . creating *life*!"

That got the king's attention. "Did you say *life*?" he demanded, looking directly at Igor.

In their hiding place, Scamper and Brain looked at each other in dismay. What had gotten into Igor?

"Yes, yes," Igor responded eagerly. "Thinking,

breathing life that can destroy freely all on its own."

"No Evil Scientist has ever been able to create life!" the king said, grabbing Igor by the collar. "They've mutated life, ended life, blasted life into a million gooey pieces . . . but *created* life?" He pushed Igor away, awestruck by the idea. "A weapon like that would be the greatest Evil Invention of all time!"

"And its inventor the greatest Evil Scientist of all time?" Igor asked hopefully.

"Of course!" the king exclaimed. "This is what I've been waiting for. And it's your job to make sure nothing happens to Glickenstein, or I'll throw you down the Recycling chute and use your hunch as a footstool."

As soon as he was gone, Scamper popped out of hiding and slapped Igor hard across the face. "Ow!" Igor cried. "What's wrong with you?"

"That's for having a death wish," Scamper said. "That's *my* thing!"

"No, Scamper, I'm not going to die." Igor wandered over to the window and stared out at the Killiseum, the site of the Evil Science Fair. Lightning crackled as Igor raised a fist with a gleam of confidence in his eyes. "For the first time ever, I'm going to *live*!"

FOUR

Igor took Scamper and Brain down to a room in the castle basement that was tucked under the stairs behind a hidden door.

"I sometimes come down here to think," he explained as he let them in.

He pulled a chain to turn on the bare bulb hanging overhead. Scamper glanced around, not looking very impressed. "Wow, how interesting," he said. "What's next? Are you going to pull out a guitar and play us a song you wrote in college about being misunderstood?"

Igor ignored Scamper's comments as he closed the door. Suddenly Scamper and Brain screamed. Hanging on the back of the door was a huge, limp, monstrous creature!

Igor glanced at it and shrugged. "It's not done yet."

This creature was his latest invention: a monster

he planned to bring to life. It was enormous, built out of whatever spare parts he could get his hands on. Once Scamper and Brain got over their initial fright, they helped him carry the monster up to the lab in pieces, laying them out on a large table.

Now that Dr. Glickenstein wasn't around anymore, there was no need to hide beneath the stairs. Igor pulled his plans out of the canister and spread them out on the desk. He grew hopeful that with the whole lab at his disposal, he might be able to finish in time for the Evil Science Fair!

The first thing Igor had to do was make minor adjustments to some of the parts he was using. He lined up several big glass jars. Each jar was filled with bubbling liquid and contained an organ. Holding a vial filled with a secret potion, he stood in front of the first jar, which was marked HEART.

Drip! Igor dribbled a bit of potion into the jar. The heart inside bulged and expanded, quickly growing to ten times its former size.

Igor smiled before moving on to the next jar, which held a pair of lungs. *Drip!* The lungs grew in size as well.

Igor continued down the row, carefully pouring a few drops of potion into each jar. He was about to add the potion into the last jar in line when Brain grabbed the vial, trying to help. Instead, he knocked the jar off the table. *Crash!* It exploded on the hard stone floor, into a mess of glass fragments and still-bubbling liquid. The organ inside was ruined.

"Nice going, Brain," Igor said, annoyed. "I guess I'm building a girl monster now!"

But that mishap couldn't keep Igor down. By the time the countdown clock read 5 DAYS UNTIL THE EVIL SCIENCE FAIR, the monster was really starting to come together. Over the next couple of days, Igor worked nonstop. He put the giant organs in their proper spots. He welded the body parts together. He lowered the enormous brain into the tremendous skull.

When all that was done, Igor carefully injected another super-secret potion into the creature's huge foot. The skin of the foot began to turn a steely gray. Slowly the gray color seeped upward, first through the leg, then down the other leg, and then up through the torso and down the arms. Soon the monster's entire body was gray.

Igor couldn't wait to find out if that part of his plans had worked. Picking up a ray gun, he shot the monster in the foot. The ray beam bounced off the steely gray skin, ricocheting off and disintegrating Scamper nearby.

Perfect, thought Igor. His monster was coming together

nicely. And by the time Scamper came to life again, Igor was tightening the last couple of bolts on his creation's neck. Then he stepped back. A glance at the clock showed that it was now 3 DAYS UNTIL THE EVIL SCIENCE FAIR.

Igor put on a radiation mask and handed one to Brain. Scamper had no need for one.

"And now," Igor said proudly, "the crucial last piece, the source of all the monster's power: the Evil Bone."

He walked over to a box that was emitting an ominous glow. Using a pair of tongs, he carefully fished something out of the box. It was an electronic bone that pulsed and glowed.

"I have to hurry," Igor muttered. "It is very sensitive to light." With the skill of a surgeon, he slid the Evil Bone into a hole he'd left in one of his monster's fingers. Then he screwed on the fingertip, which hid the evil glow.

"That's it," he said, removing his mask. "Only one thing left to do. . . ." Lightning flashed dramatically outside. With the confidence of an Evil Scientist, Igor ordered, "Pull the switch!"

He waited, staring at the monster. Nothing happened. He glanced over at Scamper, who was glaring at him. The rabbit's paw was nowhere near the switch.

"Do *not* yell at me!" Scamper said.

"Sorry. I was just . . . ," Igor replied, then sighed. "Pull the switch," he said again. *"Please?"*

Scamper smiled. "That's better."

"Wait!" Brain cried before Scamper could do anything. "Why does *he* get to pull it?"

"Because *I'm* not an idiot, *Brian*," Scamper retorted.

"My name is not Brian!" Brain protested angrily.

Scamper smirked. "Then you must have his jar."

"Stop!" Igor slapped his hands to his head. "You can *both* pull the switch."

"So there!" Brain gloated. He grabbed hold of the switch beside Scamper's paw.

"On the count of three," Igor said. "One . . . two . . ."

Scamper pulled the switch before Igor finished counting. "Hey!" Brain shrieked. "No fair!"

ZAP! Electricity surged quickly through the monster's skull, sizzling and sparking. After a few seconds Igor cut the current. Then, holding his breath, he watched his creation. Scamper and Brain stopped bickering to stare at the monster too.

But the huge creature on the table didn't move a muscle.

Igor's heart sank. The truth finally settled over him like the dark clouds that covered Malaria. "I don't believe it," he blurted out, devastated. "I'm a failure. I'm . . . an Igor!"

His whole body drooped as he stared at the cold stone floor. He couldn't look at the biggest mistake of his life.

"Get rid of that thing," Igor told his friends, turning to leave the lab. "I never want to see it again."

"Uh, funny you should say that," Scamper said in an odd tone.

Curious, Igor turned around. Scamper and Brain were staring at an empty table. The monster had disappeared!

"Igor," Brain said, sounding scared, "where did your monster go?"

Igor gulped. "I don't know, Brain."

Suddenly Scamper's eyes widened. "May I suggest looking behind you?" he said.

Igor and Brain screamed and whirled around. But there was nothing there.

Scamper shrugged. "It was just a suggestion."

The three of them huddled together in the middle of the lab, scanning all corners of the room and waiting nervously for something to happen. Every flash of lightning created creepy shadows on the walls. Every whimper of fear from Brain made Igor jump in fright.

"Maybe it just . . . spontaneously combusted," Igor said.

The trio started to relax a little, when they heard a

strange scraping noise overhead. Igor, Scamper, and Brain stood very still before slowly tilting up their heads.

Igor's monster was hanging by her arms from a ceiling beam. She swung her huge legs wildly, then did a clumsy aerial flip. A second later she landed in front of them with a castle-shaking *WHOMP!*

Igor and his friends clung to one another, frozen with terror. The monster blinked at them with her big, crazed eyes. Then her huge face spread into a deranged smile. Suddenly she screamed at the top of her giant lungs, *"Aiiiiiiiii!"*

The next second she turned and ran, her massive arms flailing. She was heading straight for the solid stone castle wall. A second later she crashed through it as if it were a sheet of paper and disappeared into the darkness, leaving only a huge, monster-shaped hole behind her.

"I did it," Igor said in fear-tinged wonder. "I created life."

Brain looked hurt as he stared at the hole in the wall. "She didn't even say snarfog!"

FIVE

Igor and Scamper burst out of the castle and looked around in panic. It was dark and stormy, as usual, but by the lightning flashes, they could see a trail of destruction leading down the forested mountainside.

"Come on!" Igor sprinted down the mountain. Scamper and Brain hurried after him.

They followed the path of crushed, broken tree limbs and giant footprints until they reached a clearing. There they saw the ruins of a once-grand cathedral. There was a sign outside.

"'Home for Blind Orphans,'" Igor read aloud. The sound of screaming children pierced the night. Igor's eyes widened in horror. "Oh, no, she's killing blind orphans! That's so *evil*!" He paused to think about what he had said. "Uh, which is great. But . . . *blind orphans*!"

The screams grew louder and louder, sending chills down the spines of Igor and Scamper. Igor feared the worst as they burst into the cathedral.

But they were not at all prepared for what they saw: Clutched in each of the monster's giant hands were several blind children. They were screaming with delight as she spun in a circle like some kind of huge, hideous whirligig. The monster herself grinned goofily at each squeal of glee.

Finally she set the orphans down carefully. They jumped up and down and clapped.

"I want to go again!" one cried.

"Me too! Me too!" another added.

"I wonder what diabolical deed she has planned next," Scamper observed with disdain. "Piggyback rides? Hopscotch?"

An old blind woman standing nearby heard him and hobbled over. "Your very large friend is a sweetheart," she told Igor.

"No, she's not," Igor snapped. What was going on? His monster wasn't acting very evil at all! He took a step toward his creation and cleared his throat. "I am your master!" he called up to her. "I command you to stop this gesture of goodwill right now and put those orphans down."

The monster looked confused. Igor lowered his own hands to the ground, trying to show her what he meant.

"Down," he repeated firmly.

The monster reluctantly set the children down. They groaned with disappointment, but Igor ignored them.

"Okay," he told the gigantic creature. "Now you're going to march right back to the castle—"

Igor stopped as the monster suddenly lunged forward. Brain screamed, making some of the orphans jump. Igor dropped to the floor. He lay there quaking with fear, waiting for one of her big, meaty hands to close over him and crush him to a pulp.

But the monster didn't grab him. Instead, she reached over him, and Igor heard a rustle. The old blind woman heard it too.

"Those are paper flowers the orphans sell," she said. "Sounds like someone likes them."

Igor couldn't believe it. His monster was gazing at one of the paper flowers, mesmerized. This was *not* what he'd had in mind at all!

"They're a buck apiece," the old woman added briskly, holding out her hand. "Buck fifty and I throw in an orphan."

Back at Castle Glickenstein, a dark carriage was hidden within a grove of twisted, ugly trees. An Igor ran up to it, panting with excitement.

"Master, I looked inside," he said in his Igor slur. "I didn't see anyone. But that's not all—"

"Yes, it *is* all," Dr. Schadenfreude said dismissively. "Because your voice annoys me. Now to break in and steal the plans to Glickenstein's invention."

Schadenfreude and Jaclyn climbed out of the carriage. When they walked up to the castle, they soon saw what the Igor had been trying to tell them. There was a huge hole in the castle wall!

They stepped through it into Dr. Glickenstein's lab. "What did this?" Jaclyn wondered, staring at the hole.

"Um, I'm guessing something big," Dr. Schadenfreude replied sarcastically. Then his eyes lit up. He hurried over to Dr. Glickenstein's desk. "Something like *this*!"

"Life?" Jaclyn said in amazement, as the two of them examined the plans that Igor had left on the desk. "Glickenstein invented life?"

Dr. Schadenfreude rubbed his chin thoughtfully. "Somehow, I don't think *he* had a hand in it." Leaning over, he picked up Dr. Glickenstein's robotic hand, which was lying forgotten on the floor.

Jaclyn glanced at the hand, then gestured to the giant hole in the wall. "Okay, so if he's dead, who invented *that*?"

But Dr. Schadenfreude barely heard her as he stared in shock at the signature at the bottom of the plans. "I don't believe it," he spat out. "Igor!"

Jaclyn laughed. "Wow," she said. "So not only is every other Evil Scientist smarter than you . . . an Igor is too? Ouch!"

Dr. Schadenfreude glared at her. "'Smart' is not mouthing off to the man who's going to become king," he warned with an evil gleam in his eyes.

It was an hour or two later when Igor finally managed to get his monster back to the lab. He lured her there by using a trail of the orphans' paper flowers. Armed with a huge bouquet of flowers, she happily reached down to grab the last one from the floor.

Igor stared at her thoughtfully. "Okay," he said. "Clearly her Evil Bone wasn't activated when she came to life."

"Ooh! Ooh!" Brain cried, raising his robotic arm eagerly. "I have an idea!"

Igor looked at him skeptically. Brain hardly ever had ideas—at least not good ones.

"Is it about *this* situation?" Igor asked.

"No," Brain said.

Igor sighed. "Is it even an idea?"

"Is French fries an idea?" Brain asked.

Scamper ignored Brain. "So how *do* you activate it?" he asked Igor, pointing toward the monster, who was still playing with her paper flowers.

Igor was pretty sure he already had the answer to that question. "We need to kick-start it," he mused. "We just need to get her to commit one act of evil."

"*Pfft,*" Scamper scoffed. "She wouldn't hurt a fly."

Just then Igor spotted a housefly buzz past and land on a table. "Okay, monster," he said to his creation. "Kill that fly!"

He pointed at the fly. But the monster looked confused.

"I said *kill* that fly," Igor repeated. When the monster just stared at the fly, he slammed his fist into his other palm. "Kill it!" he shouted. "Kill it! Kill it, girl! Come on! You're a killer! Maim it, wound it, insult it, *something*! Kill it! Kill it! Kill, kill, kill!"

The monster's face hardened. She made a fist and slammed it down. The table splintered into smithereens, and the entire lab shook.

Igor laughed and turned to Scamper. "You were saying?"

Bzzzzz! Igor stopped laughing. What was that? Turning, he saw the monster grinning sheepishly. She stepped over to the window and opened her fist, releasing the buzzing fly into the great outdoors.

"No, no, no!" Igor cried, ready to tear out his hair. "You're evil!" He pointed at her. "Evil! *Evil!*"

The monster pointed to herself. "Eva," she said.

"What?" Igor shook his head. "No, you're not Eva. . . ."

She was smiling now, seemingly pleased with her new name. "Eva," she repeated. "Eva!"

"What now, genius?" Scamper asked dryly.

"Well, thank you for asking," Brain said. "What we are going to do first is—"

Scamper kicked him away. "Go soak your brain, *Brian.*"

Suddenly a lightbulb went off over Igor's head. "That's actually not a bad idea," he said.

SIX

Igor, Scamper, Brain, and Eva entered the reception area of the local Brain Wash. A fly-headed man was working the front desk.

"Next!" a high-pitched voice called out.

Igor stepped forward, pulling Eva with him. Before leaving the castle, he'd disguised her as best he could. An entire bolt of cloth was wrapped around her head and face. Most of the rest of her was draped in an enormous blue tarp. She looked like an old peasant woman. A very, very large old peasant woman.

"Hi," Igor said to the fly-headed clerk. "I'd like to—"

"Who are you talking to?" the high-pitched voice said. "*I'm* the head guy here!"

A tiny fly buzzed up into Igor's face. Igor peered at it. The fly had the head of a man.

"Oh, sorry," Igor told the man-headed fly.

The fly stared at Eva. "What is *this*?" he demanded.

Igor was ready for the question. He'd already made up a story on the way over. After all, the last thing he wanted was for anyone to find out the truth about Eva before the Evil Science Fair!

"It's my Aunt Eva," he told the fly. "She's getting a little sweet in her old age, so I want to evil her up a bit."

He studied the sign over the desk. At the top, it read BRAINWASH TREATMENTS. Below that was the list of services offered at this place: ARSONIST, BLACK LUNG WASH, AX MURDERER, and more.

"How about the 'Ax Murderer' brainwash?" Igor suggested.

The man-headed fly looked impressed. "She must be very special to you," he said in a hushed tone.

Soon Igor and Eva were in one of the brainwashing rooms. It was fairly small, and it looked even smaller with Eva in it. There was a blank screen on one wall and a small table that held only a single remote control device.

Igor barely had time to look around before a pair of robotic clamps popped out of the wall and pried open Eva's eyes. Then two round metal brainwashers dropped out of the ceiling, aimed themselves at her head, and started pulsing.

Eva hardly seemed to notice. She had just spotted the remote control and reached for it.

"Don't touch that!" the fly scolded immediately. "It's a very complicated system. One wrong button and you'll just be watching regular cable. You want to waste your nephew's money like that?"

He buzzed over and pressed a button on the remote. The TV screen on the wall lit up. Images started flashing on it, faster and faster—horrible images of scary-looking people wielding bloody axes while victims screamed in terror. Eva stared at it, mesmerized.

Whew! Igor felt better already. Once the brainwashing was complete, he would have that Evil Science Fair prize in the bag! He stepped out of the room and found Scamper and Brain waiting for him.

"I feel like I'm sending my kid off to school for the first time," Igor told them proudly. "You know, to learn how to murder."

Igor and Scamper watched Eva's room move off on a huge conveyor belt. Then they wandered off toward the waiting room, not noticing that Brain wasn't with them.

Brain went over to the man-headed fly. "Could you

squeeze me in for a brainwash, too?" he asked. "A nice thorough scrubbing."

The fly stared at him. "What are you, an idiot?"

"Yes. Yes, I am," Brain replied proudly. "That's Latin for 'brain,' correct?" He pointed to the label on his jar.

The fly glanced at it and shrugged. "Take *Brian* to room number four," he told his fly-headed assistant.

In the waiting room, Scamper browsed through the Brain Wash's selection of greeting cards. Igor was sitting nearby watching him.

Scamper picked up a card. "Wish you weren't there," he read out loud. "This card teleports your enemy to you so you can destroy him in person." He rolled his eyes and tossed the card back on the rack. "Call me old-fashioned, but what happened to cards that just blew your head off?"

"Just think, Scamper," Igor mused happily. "In a few short moments, I'm going to have the most evil invention of all time. *Me.*"

Scamper picked up another card. "Happy Mother's Day," he read. Then he opened it.

KABOOOOOM! The card exploded, blasting Scamper's head right off his body and making everyone in the waiting room jump. Scamper's body was still for a moment until its head grew back.

Then Scamper smiled. "That's what I'm talking about," he said. "Simple, elegant, classic."

Meanwhile Brain was sitting in a tub of soapy water in one of the Brain Wash rooms. The fly-headed clerk was scrubbing him with a brush.

"You've seen a lot of brains, right?" Brain asked the clerk. "Mine's bigger than average, right? No? Hello? Can you even talk?" Annoyed by the clerk's silence, he muttered, "Guess I'll just watch TV."

He grabbed the remote from the table beside his tub, but it slipped out of his hand and splashed into the water. Brain fished it out and tried again, but no matter how many times he hit the button, nothing happened. Even Brain was smart enough to figure out that the soapy water must have ruined it.

"Great," he said with a sigh, before telling the clerk, "Hold on."

While the fly-headed assistant waited, Brain hopped out of the tub and headed for the door. He needed to find a working remote control. Once outside, he opened the door to another brainwash room. It turned out to be Eva's. The huge creature was still staring at her TV as horrible images flashed on the screen.

"You don't need this," Brain told her, grabbing her remote control and heading back to his room. He hopped into the tub, being careful not to drop the remote this time. Then he started punching the buttons again. But nothing happened.

"Aw, come on!" he cried in frustration.

Click! Click! Click! But no matter how many times he hit the buttons, his TV screen stayed dark and silent.

Meanwhile, over in Eva's room, the TV images of ax murderers faded and were replaced with a woman waterskiing. *Click!* A cake being covered in icing. *Click!* Dancers doing the twist at a poolside party.

Back in his room, Brain finally got fed up. "Stupid remote!" he cried, flinging it to the floor.

In Eva's room, the TV stopped on an image of two people sitting in director's chairs on an otherwise empty theater stage. One of the people was an attractive, elegantly dressed woman. The other was a rather stout, tweedy, serious-looking man in a suit.

"To plumb the depths of Blanche DuBois in *Streetcar* is the greatest challenge for any modern actress . . . ," the man intoned in a very serious voice.

Eva's eyes widened even farther. She stared fixedly at the screen, completely captivated by what she was seeing.

SEVEN

Igor and Scamper paced anxiously in the pickup area of the Brain Wash. "Our evil bun should be out of the oven soon," Igor said.

At that moment the fly-headed clerk stepped out of a nearby door. Brain rolled out after him. He was sparkling clean but looked a bit dizzy.

Scamper wrinkled his nose. "What's that smell?"

"Dead Dog," Brain told him. "It was either that or Wint-o-green. I think I chose wisely."

The clerk gestured toward Eva's door, and Igor's heart thumped. All his dreams were about to come true!

"I don't hear anything," he said as he turned the doorknob. He peered inside. Eva was slumped on the floor, her head down. As Igor approached his creation, she lifted her head.

"GRRRRRRRRRAAAAAAAAAAAH!" she howled, before slumping down again.

"Aaahh!" Igor, Scamper, and Brain yelled as they jumped back in fright.

"I think it worked," Scamper added.

Eva let out another roar. *"GRRRRRRAAAAAAAAAH!"*

Igor winced, his ears ringing. "Maybe they did too much?"

Eva spun around, gazing at him with interest. "Was it? Was I too much?" she asked with a wry smile. "I was pushing, wasn't I? It was only a vocal exercise, but that is a beginner's mistake. I have to own that. That's just where I am."

Igor stared at her. Then he glanced at his friends, who looked perplexed.

Eva was still talking. "Ooh!" she exclaimed. "If only I knew whether I had the 'it' factor. But how can you know? I mean, you can't learn that, you just have to be born with it." She laughed and fluttered one meaty steel-gray hand around playfully. "Oh, listen to me going on and on about me, me, me. Let's talk about you, Igor. Do *you* think I have the 'it' factor?"

Igor's jaw dropped. What was going on?

Then he noticed Eva's TV screen. The tweedy man was

clutching the attractive woman's hand, tears rolling down his plump cheeks.

"Let us thank our guest," he said between sobs. "She has taught us . . . in just one hour . . . a lifetime's worth of lessons in acting."

"Acting?" Igor repeated in disbelief. "Who—who changed the channel? Wait, where's the remote?"

He stared around desperately. Brain looked guilty.

Suddenly the man-headed fly buzzed in. "Move it," he said. "I need this room."

"No! Wait!" Igor protested. He pointed at Eva, who was playing with her hair. "We need to un-brainwash her!"

"No can do, pal," the fly replied. "Every wash comes with a sealant guaranteed to last a lifetime." It was obvious that Igor's predicament was *not* his problem. "In other words, buzz off!"

Igor was still in a daze as they headed home in Dr. Glickenstein's carriage. Being too big for the carriage, Eva rode in a trailer that Igor had hooked up behind it. She happily practiced vocal exercises while Igor fretted about what to do.

"I need a box of biscuits," she intoned. "A box of mixed biscuits. I need . . . a box of mixed biscuits." She pronounced each word very carefully—and loudly.

Igor tried hard not to listen. "It's just failure after failure," he muttered as he drove along the gloomy and winding road.

"After failure, after failure," Scamper added helpfully. When Igor gave him a look, the rabbit shrugged. "Sorry. I thought we were counting off all your failures."

"Stop the carriage!" Eva yelled suddenly.

Igor immediately yanked back on the reins. "What's the matter?" he cried as the carriage skidded to a stop.

"I don't mean to be a prima donna," Eva said calmly, "but I think I need a bigger trailer."

Igor sighed in frustration. "After failure, after failure . . . ," he repeated, not bothering to respond to Eva.

Cracking the whip, Igor sent the carriage creaking into motion again. It rumbled onward over the rough mountain road.

As he drove, he didn't notice that they were being followed. On the roof of the second carriage, Dr. Schadenfreude peered through the scope of a shrink-ray gun.

"That monster is about to be mine!" he exclaimed.

"Oh, really?" Jaclyn stuck her head out the window. "How?"

Dr. Schadenfreude smirked. "Oh, with a little some-

48

thing I happened to steal for the occasion."

"A shrink ray?" Jaclyn said in disgust, peering up at him. "Oh, *that's* a genius plan for stealing a monster!"

"I shrink the monster, make it easy to capture, and then enlarge it later." Dr. Schadenfreude aimed the ray gun at Igor's carriage. "Say hello to my little friend, because you are about to become my *little* friend."

Just as the Evil Scientist squeezed the trigger, a deer jumped onto the road in front of Igor's carriage. Igor screamed and swerved.

Zzzzap! The shrink ray hit the deer, shrinking it to the size of a mouse.

"Did I hit it?" Igor cried, leaning forward and looking around for the deer. "I hope I didn't hit it!"

Scamper rolled his eyes. "You, sir, really put the 'evil' in Evil Scientist."

As Igor straightened up, he caught a glimpse of the other carriage in the rearview mirror. He could see that an Igor was driving, and that there was a ray gun on the roof. But he couldn't tell who was manning it.

"What the . . . ?" he muttered in surprise.

His eyes widened when he saw the ray gun pointing directly at his carriage. He pulled hard on the reins again— just in time.

Zzzap! This time the beam hit a tree. It shrank down into a tiny plant.

"Aaaargh!" Dr. Schadenfreude screamed. Then he fired again—just as a moose appeared.

Zzzap! The shrink ray hit the moose.

"What is this, a nature preserve?" Dr. Schadenfreude exclaimed. The scientist had not anticipated that his plan would take such an agonizingly long time to complete!

Meanwhile Scamper and Brain were doing their best to hold on as Igor swerved back and forth on the road. "Pull over!" Brain cried. "I'm getting jar sick!"

"Someone's trying to shoot us!" Igor shouted.

Back in her trailer, Eva looked out to see what was going on. "Paparazzi!" she spat out in annoyance. "Why can't those vultures leave me alone?"

The carriages hurtled down the road at top speed as Dr. Schadenfreude kept firing. *Zzzap!* The shrink ray hit a bridge over a deep chasm just ahead. It was too late to stop. So Igor pushed the carriage on even faster.

"You're not gonna . . . ," Scamper began.

"Hold on!" Igor shouted.

The carriage was going so fast that it zoomed right over the edge—and all the way across! It landed on the far side of the chasm with a jolt.

Eva held on as she was jostled around in her trailer. "This is the worst car service I've ever used," she grumbled.

Amazingly, Dr. Schadenfreude's carriage managed to get across as well. He aimed again. He was determined not to miss his mark one more time.

"No more Doctor Nice Guy," he snarled.

This time he shrank a tunnel just ahead. Igor raced forward, trying to get through it before it got too small. He made it . . . sort of. The carriage popped out the other end and spun wildly, skidding along the road completely out of control!

Meanwhile, Dr. Schadenfreude was still coming. Igor glanced back and gulped. He wasn't going to be able to swerve out of the way forever. What could he do now?

Suddenly he had an idea—a brilliant one, in fact. "Who wants to be a big movie star?" he called out just as the ray gun fired again.

"I do!" Eva sang out, eagerly raising her hand. It stuck out of the roof of her trailer just in time for the shrink ray's beam to hit it.

The ray beam ricocheted off her hand and zapped right back at Dr. Schadenfreude. Seconds later the scientist, Jaclyn, the carriage, and the Igor had all shrunk down to the size of mice.

"Ha!" Igor cried triumphantly, watching through the side window.

But when he turned back around, he let out a scream. His carriage was careening toward the edge of a cliff—and it was far too late to stop!

The carriage plunged halfway over the edge before it miraculously came to an abrupt halt. Igor, Scamper, and Brain were thrown out the front. Scamper grabbed the carriage with one paw and Igor with the other. Igor caught Brain, who was screaming loudly. They just hung there like that for a moment, trying not to look down at the thousand-foot drop below.

EiGHT

Igor stared up at Scamper. The undead rabbit was the only thing keeping him and Brain from plunging into the abyss.

"This would be the right time to curb your suicidal tendencies," he told Scamper. Beyond the rabbit, Igor could see that Eva's trailer was still on top of the cliff. Her immense weight was holding the carriage back from falling . . . so far.

Even as the thought crossed his mind, the carriage teetered and slipped a little. Igor and his friends screamed louder than ever.

Then the carriage suddenly stopped—and miraculously it slid back up! Igor looked up to see a giant arm pulling the carriage back onto the top of the cliff. It was Eva! His monstrous creation had saved them.

Soon all of them were safely back on the road. Igor let out a sigh of relief. He was alive!

"Thank you," he told Eva sincerely.

"You're very welcome," she replied.

"You . . . you saved my life," Igor said, marveling at the irony. He had created her life, and now she had saved his.

Eva smiled. "As an actor I feel things very deeply and treasure all of life," she said sincerely. Then she started humming and swaying, dancing to her own music.

"It's actually *me* you should thank," Brain told Igor proudly. "I was the one who changed the channel on her brainwash."

"What?" Igor cried.

"Yep." Brain sounded very pleased with himself. "And if she had been evil, she would have let us all die, so technically I'm the one who saved us. But no need to thank me." He paused, considering his words. "Actually, a thank-you would be nice. It could be in the form of a card or a poem, your choice." He paused again, before finally stating, "I also like ponies."

Igor didn't need to stop to think. Instead, he calmly reached into the carriage and pulled out an ax.

"Wait, an ax?" Brain asked, confused. "I don't want an ax. Why would you offer me an ax?"

Igor took a deep breath. "You made my monster an actress!" he shrieked at the top of his lungs.

Brain screamed and bolted. Igor chased after him, waving the ax over his head.

That got Eva's attention. She stopped to watch beside Scamper.

"What play are they rehearsing?" she asked him.

"It's called *Brain Dead*," Scamper replied. "It's gonna be a smash."

Brain raced over and hid behind Eva. "Don't let him kill me!" he sobbed.

But by that time Igor's fury had worn off. He dropped the ax and collapsed into a heap of despair.

"The only thing killed here is my dream," he moaned.

Eva gasped. Then she began clapping furiously.

"Bravo! Bravo!" she cried. "Oh, you guys are so lucky to have work. If only I had a role I could really sink my teeth into."

Igor snapped his head up. That was it! Maybe his dream wasn't dead after all. It was sort of like Scamper, coming to life again and again.

"Eva," Igor said eagerly. "You're in luck. In two days there's an audition for the lead in the biggest play to hit Malaria since . . . since . . ."

"Since *The Desperate Hunchback Who Grasped at Straws*?" Scamper suggested drily.

Igor ignored him. "Seriously, Eva," he insisted, "this could be your big break!"

"Oh my gosh!" Eva's enormous face shone with nervous excitement. "I don't believe it! What play is it?"

"Play?" Igor said, trying to think quickly. Did he know any plays? "What play is it?"

"Is it a musical?" Eva asked hopefully. "So many terrific girls got their start in a musical!"

"Uh, yes, that's it," Igor agreed with relief. "It's a musical."

Eva caught her breath. "Oh . . . that's wonderful!"

She opened her mouth and sang a scale. At least that was what Igor assumed she was doing. It sounded like an earthquake when she started with the low notes, and grew into a howling hurricane in the middle. By the time she reached the high notes, the trees were shaking, the rocks were vibrating, and even the air seemed to shudder. Scamper grabbed a boulder and dropped it on his own head, crushing it. On the final, ear-shattering high note, Brain's jar cracked, and juice trickled down the outside.

"I think I just wet myself," Brain said sheepishly.

Somehow Igor had managed not to react quite so

dramatically. "Someone can sing!" he cooed.

Eva looked flattered. "Gosh," she said. "Me trying out for the lead role in a wholesome musical."

"Uh, yeah," Igor said. "Except that the main character goes nuts and battles a bunch of Evil Inventions in deadly hand-to-hand combat."

"Wow." Eva sounded impressed. "How avant-garde!"

Igor smiled at her. "Trust me," he said. "You were *born* to be in this production."

Back in the lab, Igor slouched on a director's chair and watched Eva rehearse for her "audition." As she sang, he sneaked a peek at the clock. It now had a hand-written sign pasted over part of it, so it read 2 DAYS UNTIL THE AUDITION.

Suddenly he blurted out, "No! You missed it again. Now listen, Eva—"

"Excuse me, Igor. I'm a little distracted." She took a step closer and lowered her voice. "I think the makeup girl is out to get me."

She gestured across the lab. Igor turned to look. Brain was over there, randomly mixing together some chemicals. One of the combinations started to smoke, then burst into flames.

Igor sighed. "That's Brain," he reminded Eva. "He's not the makeup girl, he's the idiot. Now try to remember: On the word 'today,' you're supposed to crush the Evil Invention to your left." He pointed to the fake Evil Invention he had mocked up for the rehearsal. It was made out of metal scraps and wire and looked a little like a deranged octopus.

"You mean 'stage left,'" Eva corrected.

Igor tried to hide his annoyance. So far they weren't making much progress on his plan. "Yes, stage left," he said. "You're supposed to smash it to smithereens."

"I know." Eva glanced at the octopus thing. "It's just . . . it looks kind of real, and it's hard because I would never hurt anything real."

"Eva, the props at the audition are going to look even more real," Igor reminded her. "Some may even scream when you smash them."

"Really?" Eva looked anxious.

"Yes. And they're also going to fight back. It's all for reality's sake." Igor added slyly, "But if you don't want to be a real actress . . ."

"No, I do, I do!" Eva protested immediately. "This is a block for me, but I'll get through it."

"Then once more from the top, please, with feeling."

Eva nodded, then hesitated again. "I just have a teeny-tiny suggestion," she said. "I know I'm not the director, but at the end of the number, I'd love to try something like this."

She drew in a breath and belted out the last line of her song. As she sang the last word, she started twirling. She twirled faster and faster until she was only a blur, like some kind of monster-sized tornado. She whirled across the lab, sending furniture and equipment flying. Then she hit a support column, smashing it to smithereens. A chunk of the ceiling came crashing down in an explosion of dust and plaster.

A second later Eva came to a stop. She landed in a split, with jazz hands, hardly seeming to notice that she was now covered in dust and debris.

Igor just stared at her for a moment. Then he broke into a huge grin. "Works for me."

NINE

Later that night Igor stood on one of the balconies of Dr. Glickenstein's castle. It was a perfect Malaria night. The entire kingdom of Malaria spread out before him, looking absolutely dark and dreary. The castles of the other Evil Scientists dotted the mountains all around, their windows glowing sickly green or bilious yellow as the scientists worked around the clock to prepare for the Evil Science Fair. On the highest mountain stood the angular, dark form of King Malbert's Royal Tower, and just beneath the cloud line was a single window in the tower. A beacon of light shot out the window, straight up into the ominous clouds hovering over the Killiseum, the site of the science fair.

Igor's heart quickened as he gazed at the Killiseum. He had looked out at this view many times before. But tonight it felt different. Soon every citizen out there in Malaria—

perhaps every citizen in the world!—would know his name.

Suddenly the balcony shook and Igor steadied himself against the wall. Eva stepped outside, wrapped in a bathrobe, with a scarf around her throat. She held a teacup carefully in her massive hands.

"Great work today, Eva," Igor told her. "You took some really big steps."

"Thank you, Igor," Eva whispered. "I'm whispering to protect my voice. I couldn't have done it without you."

Igor turned back to look out at the city below. "Isn't it beautiful?" Noting the beam of light in the Royal Tower, he added, "King Malbert has turned this country into a paradise. His tower shines out for all the world to see as a beacon of Evil."

Eva's face took on an expression of slight bewilderment. "And that's . . . a good thing?"

Igor smiled at her indulgently. Without her Evil Bone functioning properly, she couldn't be expected to understand these things. But he was sure she'd catch on as soon as she did something truly evil. And after their latest rehearsal, he was sure that wouldn't be long.

"We were a nothing country until King Malbert taught us that the way to succeed is by doing evil," he explained patiently.

"This is a tough town," Eva said.

Igor shrugged. "In this world, nice guys finish last."

"So I have to step on people to get ahead?" Eva asked, sounding a little sad.

Igor glanced down at his feet, suddenly uncomfortable with the way the conversation was going. "Uh, yeah," he muttered.

Eva shook her head. "Well, I'd rather be a good nobody than an evil somebody. And so would you." She jabbed one huge finger at Igor. "Because you're good, Igor."

"Don't say that," Igor said.

"It's true." Eva beamed at him. "You *are* good. You've helped me with my audition. You made me this delicious tea. You're a very good friend."

"Evil Scientists don't have friends."

"Well, what are Brain and Scamper?"

Igor snorted. "Headaches!"

"Oh." Eva looked a bit crestfallen. "Is that all I am too?"

"No," Igor replied quickly.

"Okay." Eva seemed satisfied. "Then you can be my number two friend."

"Number two?" Igor repeated, surprised to feel a twinge of jealousy. "Who's your number one friend?"

Eva smiled impishly. "See? You're jealous," she teased. "You *do* want to be my friend!"

Igor relaxed. His monster had a sense of humor! It wasn't something one normally found in an Evil Invention. Still, he couldn't help smiling back.

Not far from the Royal Tower, a Malarian TV personality named Carl Cristall was in his studio recording that night's show. Cristall was invisible and hosted a popular talk show called *Cristall Clear.*

He stood in front of a large screen showing some grainy black-and-white footage of dark rain clouds rolling across the sky. The cameras framed him from the waist up, but because he was invisible, all the audience could see of him was his flashy, expensive-looking shirt and tie.

"Hi, I'm Carl Cristall," he began in his schmoozy TV-personality voice, "and tonight on *Cristall Clear* my guest is King Malbert, mastermind of Malaria's evil response to the clouds."

King Malbert was already sitting in one of the interview chairs on the set. As Cristall came over and prepared to sit down across from him, the king's eyes widened in alarm. Cristall was wearing a shirt and tie, and he also had on shoes and socks. But there was nothing in between.

"Welcome, Your Highness," Cristall said. As he took his seat in the vinyl chair, it let out a definite squeak.

"You're . . ." The king gulped. "Uh, not wearing any pantaloons!"

"Hmm?" Cristall was obviously unconcerned. "Oh, no, I'm not. I figure, why does an invisible man need to wear pants? It's very liberating."

There was another loud squeak as Cristall shifted in his chair. The king shuddered.

"Sire," Cristall said briskly. "The clouds—were they a blessing or a curse?"

The king did his best to focus on the interview instead of his host's lack of pants. "Well, of course I would never wish the clouds on my people," he said. "But we rallied together for the common good by embracing evil, and look at us now! Respected, successful . . ." He trailed off before suddenly exclaiming, "What are you doing?"

Cristall's shirt sleeve was moving. He appeared to be scratching something.

"Just scratching my leg," Cristall replied. "Sire, the Evil Science Fair is just two days away. Predictions? Can anyone beat Dr. Schadenfreude?"

King Malbert pursed his lips. "Well, I hate to predict," he said. "All the Evil Scientists are twisted fiends in their own

Igor was destined to be like all Igors in Malaria—except that he was already the proud inventor of Brain, Scamper, and a soon-to-be-evil monster.

The switch was **pulled**, and Igor's monster was born . . . but she was not at all evil!

The monster was sent to the Brain Wash to become evil, but she turned into an actress instead.

Eva began rehearsing for her big role, and Igor worked hard on her costume.

Things were not looking good for Igor: King Malbert wanted to send him to the Igor Recycling Plant . . .

and Dr. Schadenfreude convinced Eva that Igor had someone else in mind for the big role.

Meanwhile Igor discovered that the darkness over Malaria had been a big lie.

With the truth revealed, Malaria was a different place. The sun shone every day—and it always would.

right." His eyes took on a dark gleam. "That said, there may be a genius this year with an evil invention so revolutionary that Schadenfreude may finally get . . ." He paused and moved his hands in a complicated mime action.

"Scuba-diving lessons?" Cristall guessed, sounding puzzled.

"No!" the king said, annoyed. "Knocked off his perch!"

In Castle Schadenfreude, as in much of Malaria, the TV was tuned to Carl Cristall's show. Thanks to a stolen growth ray, Dr. Schadenfreude, his Igor, and Jaclyn had returned to their normal sizes. Now the Evil Scientist was glowering at the image of King Malbert on the screen.

"The only one getting knocked off his perch is *you*," Dr. Schadenfreude growled as he clenched his fists. "I need that monster! I will not be beaten by a hunchbacked, pot-bellied, bulgy-eyed runt!"

"I think he's kind of cute," Jaclyn commented. When the scientist gave her a nasty look, she simply shrugged. "Talent is attractive."

Dr. Schadenfreude fumed in his chair as she left the room. "I can just picture it now," he muttered. "That Igor and his monster, plotting their deadly combat maneuvers. . . ."

At that moment Igor was bent over his desk, looking even more hunchbacked than usual as he sketched furiously, his mouth twisted into a grimace. When Eva came in, he glanced up. Then he picked up his sketch and showed it to her.

Eva clapped with delight. It was a sketch of an amazing costume—just for her!

Everyone at Dr. Glickenstein's castle was hard at work preparing for the Evil Science Fair—uh, audition. Eva was enthusiastically rehearsing almost nonstop, stomping with growing relish on the props that Igor built.

Scamper had discovered that he had a way with a needle and thread. He sewed and sewed, and Eva's costume started to come together.

By the time the clock on the wall read 1 DAY UNTIL THE AUDITION, everything was almost ready. Scamper tried some wigs on Eva, unscrewing the top of her skull and screwing on each wig in turn.

Later Eva wanted to try something new. So Igor sat at the piano, playing along with her singing. She draped herself over the piano like a singer she'd seen on TV . . . and crushed it into pieces.

At first she looked embarrassed. But then Igor smiled. Eva smiled back, looking relieved.

This whole time, Igor had been so busy, he hardly had time to think. But when he did think, it was about only one thing: All his dreams were about to come true. Soon he would be much more than a lowly Igor. He would be the winner of the Evil Science Fair. He would be lauded as a true Evil Scientist. He would be the toast of Malaria.

He could hardly wait!

TEN

"Guys, can you come in here, please?" Eva poked her head into the lab. Igor, Scamper, and Brain were putting some finishing touches on her costume. "I need to talk to you."

She disappeared back into the parlor. Igor exchanged an anxious look with his friends. What was going on now?

"If she's having a 'woman problem,' it's all yours," Scamper told Igor.

Soon the three of them were sitting on a couch in the parlor. Eva stood before them with her hands behind her back.

Then she held out her hands. In them were three objects wrapped in newspaper.

"What are these?" Igor asked.

"Opening-night presents!" Eva smiled nervously. "I know it's technically just an audition tomorrow, but I figured what the hey." She handed one gift to each of them. "They're not much since I had to use stuff I found around here, but, well . . . you first, Brain!"

Brain ripped open his package. It looked like a slim slip of paper. Written on it was the name BRAIN.

"It's a new label for your jar," Eva explained.

Brain gasped. "'Brain' is spelled right!" He paused. "It is, right?"

Eva unpeeled the label and stuck it over the old one on Brain's jar. "You shouldn't really worry about labels, though," she told him. "You may be a brain, but you have *heart*. And in some ways that's more important."

"Heart?" Brain said. "I'd kill for a pair of feet."

"Open yours, Scamper," Eva urged.

Scamper unwrapped his present. It was a small potted plant. For a moment the undead rabbit looked confused.

"It's a prehistoric evergreen," Eva said. "They live forever. I just want to make sure that if anything ever happens to the three of us, you always have company."

Scamper gulped, staring from the plant to Eva and back again. His eyes welled up.

"Great," he said, wiping his eyes as he tried to sound

69

unmoved by the gift. "Must be allergic to it. With any luck its dinosaur-era toxins will kill me." He swiped at his watery eyes again. "Can we move on to Igor now?" he added irritably.

Igor stared down at the gift in his hands. He couldn't believe Eva had done this.

"No one's ever given me a gift before," he said softly.

"It's something no director can be without," Eva said.

Igor unwrapped the gift. Inside was a flat caplike thing. He wasn't quite sure what it was supposed to be.

"It's a beret!" Eva said happily. Taking it from his hands, she placed it carefully on his head, tilting it at a rakish angle. *"Voilà!"*

Scamper rolled his eyes. "That's French for 'Please stop pelting me and my ridiculous hat with rocks,'" he said.

But Igor barely heard him. The hat felt nice on his head. It made him feel a little less . . . *lumpy*, somehow.

Just then Brain spoke up. "Hey, Igor, where's our gift for Eva?"

"Our gift?" Igor repeated.

Eva gasped. "You guys didn't!" she cried, her face glowing with anticipation.

Scamper shot Igor an evil smile. "We did," he assured Eva. "Where'd you put it, Igor?"

Igor glared at him. Scamper knew very well that they didn't have anything for Eva. But she looked so excited that there was no way Igor could admit that now. It would crush her. And that was the last thing he wanted to do, especially just twenty-four hours before she was supposed to crush all the Evil Inventions.

"It's, uh, in the other r-room," he stammered, still glaring at Scamper. Igor wanted to kill him—not that he could.

He rushed out to the lab, trying to think. What could he find that would make a good gift? He stared around in a panic. Desk chair? No. Trash can? No. Beaker full of Brain's latest disgusting concoction? No way.

Suddenly his gaze fell on something on the desk. He sighed with relief. *That* would do. . . .

A moment later Igor returned to the parlor with his hands behind his back. Eva was waiting with the others.

"Eva, we got you this," Igor announced. "It's a necklace."

He held out his hand. Dangling from it was the metal canister that had once held all his plans. He didn't really need it anymore, now that Dr. Glickenstein was gone. Besides, it seemed kind of appropriate somehow. If it wasn't for that canister, Eva might not even exist right now.

Without a word, Eva reached for it. Holding it in her

71

hands, she simply stared at it for a long time—which made Igor a little nervous. Maybe it hadn't been such a great idea after all.

"It's the most beautiful thing I've ever seen!" Eva burst out at last. "Igor, can you . . . ?" She gave him the necklace and leaned forward.

Igor carefully fastened it around her tree-trunk-like neck. It barely fit.

"I'm never going to take this off," Eva promised, engulfing the canister in one hand. "That way all of you will be close to my heart forever." Tears started to trickle down her cheeks. "I—I need to write this down in my sense-memory journal," she choked out before turning and running from the room.

Igor, Scamper, and Brain just stared after her for a moment. All of them felt a little ashamed.

With the floor still shaking from her departure, Igor struggled to sound casual. "See, this is the exact kind of moment that would be tough for someone who wasn't meant to be an Evil Scientist," he said. "Somebody who would go all soft and want to tell her the truth . . ." He looked at his friends. "Lucky for us *I'm* here, right?"

"Yeah," Scamper said, before wandering off with Brain. "Lucky us."

Igor headed outside to the courtyard just beyond the castle door. He stared off into the darkness, wondering where his excitement about the Evil Science Fair had gone all of a sudden.

"Stay on track," he muttered. "We're almost there. Just don't let her get into your head."

Glancing upward, he saw that Eva's window was lit up with a cheerful yellow glow. Her enormous silhouette moved into view, blocking out most of the light.

"Pfennig for your thoughts," a voice said from just a few feet away.

Igor jumped and whirled around. Heidi was standing there smiling at him, looking as blond and beautiful as ever. He hadn't seen her since before Dr. Glickenstein's demise.

"Heidi?" he said. "Um, Dr. Glickenstein is under the rug. Uh, I mean, under the weather."

Heidi took a step closer. "I did not come to see him," she purred. "I came to see *you*."

She smiled coyly. Igor gulped. What could gorgeous Heidi want with an Igor like him?

"Me?" he squeaked.

Upstairs, Eva happened to step over to the window at that very moment. She looked down just in time to see

Heidi move even closer to Igor. The happy smile that had been glued to Eva's face instantly faded.

So that was how it was. She should have known better than to get her hopes up. She tiptoed away from the window before Igor could look up.

Meanwhile, Igor was having trouble looking anywhere but Heidi's captivating face. She was so delicate, so pretty . . .

Heidi held out an envelope. "An Igor came by today and asked me to deliver this to you," she said.

Oh. Igor's heart sank. He should have known it was something like that.

"What is it?" he asked, taking the envelope.

She shrugged. "I haven't any idea."

Igor opened it and took out a card. He looked at the front. "'Wish you weren't there,'" he read aloud before opening it.

ZZZZZIP! A flash of light blinded him.

ZZZZAP! Just like that, Heidi stood alone in the courtyard.

ELEVEN

gor blinked, still blinded by the sudden bright flash of light. When his vision cleared, he gasped. Dr. Schadenfreude was sitting right in front of him, a cocktail in his hand. Where had he come from?

Then he looked around and realized the truth. He wasn't in his own courtyard anymore. He was standing in Dr. Schadenfreude's ballroom. The card Heidi had delivered to him was one of those stupid dematerialization cards!

"Oh, excellent, wonderful," the Evil Scientist said with a wicked smile. "You got my card."

Back at Castle Glickenstein, Heidi was still looking at the card lying on the ground when Eva came running outside. "Is everything okay?" Eva asked. "I heard a strange noise!"

Heidi stared at Eva in shock. She opened her mouth but nothing came out.

Eva suddenly felt self-conscious. "I wasn't at the door listening to you and Igor," she said a little too quickly. "I was just, um . . ." Forcing a cheery smile, she decided to change the subject. "Hi! We haven't met. I'm Eva." She stuck out one huge hand.

Heidi just stared at it. Eva waited a few seconds, then gave up and pulled it back. She searched her mind for something to say. After all, even if Igor had a girlfriend she hadn't known about, that was no reason to be rude. Besides, judging from the look on her face, the tiny little blond hadn't been expecting her, either.

"You're upset, aren't you?" Eva said. "Who is this strange woman living with Igor, right? Well, believe me, Igor and I are just friends. As his girlfriend, you have nothing to worry about."

At that, Heidi finally found her voice. "I'm not his girlfriend," she said, a little confused by the monster's outburst.

Eva tried to hide her excitement. "You're not?" she exclaimed. "But the way he looks at you . . ." She hung her head. "He never looks at me that way."

"Maybe some guys prefer girls who *don't* look like

they've been put together at the junkyard," Heidi replied, taking in Eva's mismatched parts, from her huge feet to the bolts in her massive neck.

Eva wasn't sure how to respond. Was Heidi making a joke? Or was that an insult?

"Right," she said uncertainly. "Well, I have to get some rest for my audition tomorrow. It was nice meeting you."

Feeling a little embarrassed, though she wasn't sure why, Eva ran for the door. Unfortunately she yanked on it a little too hard, pulling it completely off its hinges. Shooting a sheepish smile over her shoulder, she hurried inside.

Heidi stared after her, still a bit stunned. "Audition?" she repeated to the cold night air.

Back at Castle Schadenfreude, Igor was now sitting with the Evil Scientist in his skull-shaped Jacuzzi. Dr. Schadenfreude looked relaxed and comfortable, but Igor felt awkward as he sat there in the steaming water holding the drink the scientist's Igor had handed him. Tiki music played softly in the background, and flaming torches lined the edge of the tub.

Dr. Schadenfreude took a sip of his drink, which was in a coconut shell. "How's your cocktail, Igor?" he asked.

Igor looked down at his own coconut-shell drink. He

lifted it uncertainly, aiming the straw toward his mouth.

"Wait!" Dr. Schadenfreude held up his hand. "You should be sipping in style. Igor! Krazy Straw! Right now!"

Dr. Schadenfreude's Igor rushed in. He was dressed in Polynesian garb, with several leis draped around his hump. He quickly replaced the normal straw in Igor's drink with a long, garishly colored, twisty-turny one.

"There!" Dr. Schadenfreude smiled, looking satisfied as his Igor stepped back. "Isn't that better?"

"Excuse me, sir," Igor said in his normal voice. "But why—" Suddenly he caught himself. Clearing his throat, he shifted into his slurred Igor voice. "I mean, why am I here?"

"You can drop that slur around me," Dr. Schadenfreude said with a chuckle. "I don't even make my own Igors talk that way. Isn't that right, Igor?"

He turned to his Igor, who looked uncertain. After a moment, the Igor replied in a normal voice, "Uh, that's right, master."

The scientist shook his head, smiling and tut-tutting. "How many times do I have to tell you? Call me Frederick."

"Okay . . ." The Igor paused, looking a little nervous. "Frederick."

"I have to get back," Igor interrupted. "Dr. Glickenstein will be missing me."

"Really?" Schadenfreude said. "Because somehow, I think he's missing more than his right-hand man."

He leaned out of the tub and picked something up. Igor's eyes widened. It looked like . . . it *was* Dr. Glickenstein's robotic hand! Where had Dr. Schadenfreude gotten *that*?

A few minutes later Dr. Schadenfreude and Igor were on a pair of massage tables. The scientist's Igor was racing back and forth between the two tables, massaging first his master, then Igor, then his master again. Before long he grew dizzy.

But Dr. Schadenfreude wasn't paying any attention to him. "Look, I know all about Glickenstein and his deadness," he told Igor smugly. "I also know about your monster."

Igor raised his head, horrified. Dr. Schadenfreude knew about Eva? This was not good.

Dr. Schadenfreude smirked. "I'm going to guess your plan. You win the Evil Science Fair, and then everyone looks past the hunch thing and accepts you for the real you, you grab the girl of your dreams and cha-cha-cha your way to a happy ending." He glanced over at Igor. "Am I close?"

"No, not entirely," Igor replied. "I don't know how to cha-cha."

TWELVE

A few minutes later Igor and the Evil Scientist were wrapped in towels, lounging in a steam room. The sweat dripped down Igor's brow as Dr. Schadenfreude talked.

"We're a lot alike, Igor," he said. "I want to be more as well, but society won't let me. So here's *my* plan. I enter the Evil Science Fair with your monster and I win. Then I turn the monster on the king." A strange glint entered his eyes. "Ding-dong the king is dead; long live the *new* king: me! And then you come in as Malaria's new Evil Scientist, *Doctor* Igor. So, what do you say to that?"

Igor was stunned. "You want to overthrow the king?" he exclaimed. "But that's . . . but that's *wrong!*"

"Wrong?" Dr. Schadenfreude asked, somewhat puzzled. "I thought you wanted to be an Evil Scientist."

"I do," Igor said quickly. "But—"

"Then stop thinking like an Igor," Dr. Schadenfreude interrupted. "Evil Scientists don't let anyone stand in their way."

"They step on people to get ahead," Igor said.

"Exactly."

"She'll never do it," Igor realized suddenly.

"She?" Dr. Schadenfreude asked.

"The monster," Igor explained. "She isn't evil. Something went wrong and her Evil Bone was never activated."

The scientist frowned. He hated having problems crop up in his evil plans. It wasted so much time—time that he could spend daydreaming about what he would do once he became king.

"So how do we get this bone up and running?" Dr. Shadenfreude asked impatiently. "Do we kick it, slap it, take it to the movies, call it Irene?"

"She needs to commit an evil act," Igor said. "But since she's not evil, she won't." He almost told Dr. Schadenfreude about his plans to trick Eva into committing an evil act at the Evil Science Fair. Almost. But something told him to hold back.

Meanwhile Dr. Schadenfreude just laughed. "Well, your troubles are over," he exclaimed, sounding almost light-hearted. "I can get a woman to do absolutely anything!"

Igor was torn. In a way, what Dr. Schadenfreude was offering him made perfect sense. Hadn't he spent his whole life wishing for nothing more than to be an Evil Scientist? Still, his proposal made Igor uneasy.

"I don't know . . . ," Igor said, tugging nervously on his sweaty towel.

Dr. Schadenfreude's eyes widened in horror. "Don't tell me you have *feelings* for this thing?"

"No!" Igor snapped defensively.

"Good. Because that would be pathetic." Dr. Schadenfreude leaned forward again. "I can give you everything you've ever wanted."

Igor's mind reeled. He had never been so confused. What did he really want, anyway?

He stood up, hanging on to his towel. "I need to go."

"The Evil Science Fair is in a few hours," Schadenfreude said. "You're either with me or against me. Yes or no."

Igor paused. Dr. Schadenfreude was giving him a choice. Or was he? The Evil Scientist wasn't exactly known for his sense of fairness, and the two of them *were* trapped there in a very small room together. . . .

Suddenly feeling claustrophobic and panicky, Igor bolted for the door. It was locked!

"I'll take that as a no," Dr. Schadenfreude said, pulling

out a vaporizer. "What are you going to do now, smart guy?"

Igor thought fast. He leaped across the steam room and kicked over the steam machine.

HISSSSSSS! Steam billowed out, quickly filling the entire room in a hazy cloud of moisture. Dr. Schadenfreude could barely see the vaporizer in front of his face, but he fired anyway.

He missed Igor. The vaporizer beam hit the door instead, breaking the lock. Yanking open the door, Igor raced out of the steam room. He grabbed a bottle of massage oil and poured it all over the floor.

Dr. Schadenfreude burst out of the steam room, hot on Igor's trail. He waved his vaporizer around wildly to clear the haze drifting out after him. Then he hit the edge of the massage-oil puddle and let out a shout as he began to slip. Barely keeping his balance, the scientist skidded and slid across the floor—right to the edge of the Jacuzzi.

"Whoa!" he shouted, trying to stay upright.

Igor grabbed the Krazy Straw from his coconut drink. There was a lemon seed stuck in it. He raised the straw to his lips, took a breath, then blew hard.

PLONK! The lemon seed shot out of the straw and hit

Dr. Schadenfreude right in the chest. The Evil Scientist let out another shout, then tipped backward into the Jacuzzi with a loud splash.

Tossing the straw aside, Igor grabbed a skull candle and smashed it against the Jacuzzi's control panel, which exploded in a shower of sparks. The cover of the hot tub started to close—with Dr. Schadenfreude struggling to right himself in the bubbling water!

Dr. Schadenfreude's Igor panicked. "Frederick!" he cried, leaping into the Jacuzzi just as the cover slid shut, covering them both. All Igor could see now was the shape of the other Igor's hunch moving underneath the cover. "Frederick?" the Igor called out. "Are you all right?"

"Get off of me, you imbecile!" Dr. Schadenfreude howled, his angular shape thrashing around under the cover as well.

Igor didn't stick around any longer. He turned and raced for the door.

Back at Castle Glickenstein, Eva sat in front of a mirror and stared at her own face. She lifted a massive hand and gently touched one of the scars where Igor had stitched her together. Until she'd seen Heidi, Eva had never really paid attention to her own appearance. But now she seemed to see herself for the first time. She wasn't sure she liked what she saw.

"Okay!" Scamper said briskly as he and Brain hurried into Eva's room, pushing a mannequin with her costume draped over it. "We just finished it. I just hope it's cinched enough at the waist, and obviously, if I had more time I would have made it flare out at the knees. . . ."

Brain stared at him. "What?" Scamper said. "It's not like I'm into this at all. I had four hundred sisters."

Eva was still staring at her own reflection. "You guys are my friends," she said. "So you'll tell me the truth, right?"

"Uh, sure," Scamper said, though he really wasn't sure.

Eva paused and bit her lip before asking, "Do you think . . . I'm pretty?"

Scamper gulped and glanced at Brain. Brain stared back. Neither of them knew what to say. Who knew a huge monster could be so vulnerable?

"Brain," Scamper said at last, "get me a tub of eyeliner, a pound of lipstick . . . and if all else fails, the severed head of a supermodel!"

In the ballroom at Castle Schadenfreude, Heidi strolled toward the Jacuzzi, calmly observing the thrashing and cursing under its cover. When she reached the control panel, she studied her flawless fingernails for a long moment and then punched a button. The cover slid back, releasing Dr. Schadenfreude and his Igor from their hot, bubbling prison.

"No, please!" Schadenfreude sputtered as he climbed out. His clothes dripped with water, his voice with sarcasm. "Take your own sweet time! I loved it under there!"

"Really?" Heidi snapped back. "Then maybe you should stay down there."

"It's true," Dr. Schadenfreude said, scowling. "The dank smell of mildew reminds me of my love when I found her living on the streets!"

Offended, Heidi slapped Dr. Schadenfreude's Igor, who had just gotten out of the tub. Dr. Schadenfreude quickly slapped the Igor in return, sending him splashing back into the hot water. Then the scientist grabbed Heidi's hand to kiss it.

"Wait," Heidi told him. "No kissing Heidi."

She pulled a round pill case out of her purse and flipped it open. It was divided into thirteen compartments, each marked with a different girl's name. Heidi selected a pill out of one of the compartments and swallowed it. Almost immediately, she went into sudden violent convulsions. Her blond hair darkened, her face writhed and changed. Moments later, she had turned into Jaclyn!

Then she shot Dr. Schadenfreude a glance tinged with jealousy. "Or do you like me better as Heidi?" she asked.

Dr. Schadenfreude pretended to weigh his options. "Hmm," he said. "Jaclyn, Heidi. Jaclyn, Heidi."

Jaclyn let out a scream of frustration.

Dr. Schadenfreude wrinkled his nose. "It would be really swell if you didn't go psycho-girlfriend on me right now, all right?"

"I'm not psycho!" Jaclyn shrieked.

"Obviously not," the Evil Scientist said as soothingly as he could.

Jaclyn glared at him. "How would you feel if every day you had to be thirteen different people?" she demanded. "I'm Jaclyn, your girlfriend . . ." She opened another compartment in her pill case and threw back another pill.

Once again, she quickly changed, this time into a stunning redhead. "Then I'm Dr. Nachtmahr's girlfriend," she said. She popped another pill and became a slender blonde. "Then I'm Dr. Groaner's girlfriend . . . all for you! To help you steal inventions year after year!"

Dr. Schadenfreude nodded, looking pleased with

himself. "And I still say those stolen pills were the best invention yet."

With one more pill, Jaclyn was Jaclyn again. "Well, this time they really paid off," she said, forgetting her anger as she remembered what she had come to tell him. "Guess what I found out about our favorite little monster?" She paused and smirked. "Or should I say . . . *actress*?"

THiRTEEN

"I'm ready for my close-up, Mr. Director!" Eva sang out. Igor looked up and was instantly transfixed at the sight of Eva standing at the top of the castle staircase. She was draped in an elegant-looking gown, and her huge feet were jammed into matching high heels. Makeup had transformed her face from hideous and deformed to *much less* hideous and deformed. Her wig was carefully coiffed. She stood there for a moment, arms raised in a glamorous movie-star pose.

"Eva?" Igor gasped.

She started slowly down the stairs. But she had taken only a couple of steps when she tripped over her high heels. She stumbled down the rest of the staircase, her arms flailing.

Igor rushed forward to catch her, not really stopping to

89

think about the fact that she outweighed him by about ten to one. The two of them ended up landing face-to-face on the hard foyer floor.

"*Too* close?" Eva asked sheepishly.

"No," Igor replied, gazing at her in amazement. "Eva, you look . . . *beautiful.*"

Their eyes locked together. "This is such a cliché," Eva murmured. "The leading lady *falling* for her director."

"Well, you're not used to heels," Igor said. Then he swallowed hard, realizing that wasn't what she'd meant. "Oh. You mean . . ."

Just then Scamper and Brain stepped into view at the top of the stairs. Both of them were covered in powder and sparkles and little blotches of makeup. They looked exhausted but proud.

"Our work here is done," Brain announced.

"*Our* work?" Scamper glared at him. "You spent the entire time playing with a piece of ribbon."

Brain looked at his robotic hand. It was clutching a piece of ribbon. He giggled goofily, then started playing with it as he zoomed off. Scamper shook his head and sighed before heading after him.

But Igor wasn't paying any attention to them. He couldn't stop staring at Eva as he helped her to her feet.

Maybe it was a concussion from the tumble he'd taken when he'd tried to catch Eva, but he was starting to have second thoughts about what he had planned for her. Third thoughts, even.

"Eva, about the audition," he began. "I think I've given you the wrong direction."

Eva looked surprised. "But I feel so prepared!"

"No, I've been trying to make you play a role you're not right for."

Igor took a deep breath. What he was about to reveal could bring about the end of his dream. "I have to tell you the truth. . . ."

But before he could go any further, there came the sound of someone yodeling just outside. At least it started off as a yodel.

"A-dodle-dodle-day-ee-OWWWWWCH!"

Igor sighed heavily. Talk about timing . . .

"Heidi," he muttered. Then he told Eva, "I'll just be a moment."

He hurried outside to the courtyard. Heidi was on the ground, clutching her leg.

"My ankle!" she exclaimed with a pout. "It twisted like a pretzel, Igor!"

Meanwhile, Eva was straightening her wig and

adjusting her dress. "Enchanting!" a voice said suddenly from behind her.

Spinning around in surprise, she saw a tall, handsome man standing in the shadows. He stepped forward and shot her a dazzling smile.

"Who are you?" Eva exclaimed.

"Someone who doesn't want your unique gifts to go to waste," Dr. Schadenfreude—for it was him, of course—purred in his most charming tone.

Eva gasped. "Are you a talent agent?"

Back out in the courtyard, Igor had helped Heidi over to a bench and was sitting beside her. But strangely enough, Heidi seemed to have recovered from her injury as soon as they sat down.

"I was so worried!" she cooed with a fetching smile. "You opened that card and I thought I'd lost you forever!"

Igor gulped. A week ago—even a day ago!—he would have been overjoyed at her obvious concern. Stunned, yes, but then overjoyed after that.

But not anymore. Any feelings he'd once had for Heidi had disappeared as soon as he'd caught sight of Eva at the top of that staircase. And maybe even before that.

"Heidi," he said, "I need to tell you something—"

She didn't let him finish. "I don't know what it is," she

said, reaching over and caressing his face. "But I feel like for the first time I'm seeing the real Igor. And I think I'm in love with him."

At that moment a bolt of lightning crackled overhead. Igor smiled weakly. "Boy, when it rains, it pours."

On the other side of the castle's thick stone wall, Eva was upset by what Dr. Schadenfreude was telling her about Igor. She backed away from him, not wanting to hear any more. But the scientist kept talking.

"Igor is a liar!" Dr. Schadenfreude insisted.

"No! Igor would never lie to me," Eva cried. "Igor cares about me."

Dr. Schadenfreude laughed as if that was the funniest thing he'd heard all year. "Cares?" he exclaimed. "He doesn't care. He built you to be a weapon."

"No! You're wrong."

"He'll never look at you and see a woman." Dr. Schadenfreude stared directly into her eyes. "All he will ever see is a monster."

Stung, Eva glanced over at the mirror. "I don't believe you," she said, not sounding so sure.

"Open your eyes." Dr. Schadenfreude stepped over and drew back the curtains, revealing the dark courtyard just beyond. "Igor has someone else in mind for your role."

Eva peered out the window—just in time to see Heidi lean in and kiss Igor on the lips! She didn't want to believe what her eyes were telling her, but there was no denying it.

Dr. Schadenfreude reached out a sympathetic hand. "There's nothing more for you here," he said soothingly. "Come with me. I can make *you* a star."

Too upset to protest—or even to think—Eva pulled off the necklace Igor had given her. Then she took Dr. Schadenfreude's hand. As he led her from the room, she let the necklace fall to the floor with a clatter.

A moment later Igor pulled away from Heidi's kiss. Heidi looked surprised.

"What's wrong?" she asked.

"I can't believe I'm saying this," Igor said. "But I've made someone else. Uh, I mean I've *met* someone else. Who I made." He shrugged helplessly. "It's complicated."

Heidi's blue eyes suddenly went cold. "Wait a minute," she snapped. "*You're* rejecting *me*?"

"I'm sorry," Igor began.

"For that big bumpy thing?" she shrieked, gesturing vaguely toward Eva's room in the castle.

Igor blinked. "How do you know about—"

"I mean, I know this isn't the best-looking me, but come

94

Look at *you*!" Heidi cried. "You're hideous! And I kissed you! Ugh! Yuck!"

She pulled out a pill and tossed it down. Within seconds, she became Jaclyn. Igor's jaw dropped in surprise.

"And for a second there I thought you were actually *smart*!" Jaclyn spat out before storming off.

For a moment Igor was confused. Then his mind clicked into gear. He realized that there could be only one dastardly mind behind this evil plot.

"Schadenfreude!" he cried.

He raced back inside and called out for Eva. But there was no answer. As he ran across the foyer, his foot hit something that skittered across the floor.

He stopped and looked down. It was Eva's necklace! His heart dropped. She had sworn she would never take it off.

Before he could bend down to pick it up, several Royal Guards burst in through the front door and seized him. King Malbert strolled in after them.

"Where's Glicky?" he demanded. "And before you answer, you should know that someone sent me this."

He held up Glickenstein's robotic hand. Igor gulped. He should have known he couldn't keep the truth secret for long. He'd only hoped he could manage it until after the Evil Science Fair.

"Your Highness," he said. "He's dead."

The king glared at Igor. "And he didn't invent life, did he?" He seemed to be more concerned about the invention than about the inventor.

"No. *I* did," Igor admitted.

For a moment the king and his guards simply stared at him. Then the guards burst out laughing.

"An Igor inventing?" one of them howled in disbelief.

The other slapped his knee, bent over with mirth. "That's rich!"

"Silence!" the king thundered. He leaned closer to Igor. "Hunchy invented life, huh? Well, where is it?"

"It's a she," Igor corrected. "And, uh, I think someone's taken her."

"Well, if *she* comes back, we'll tell her where to find you." The king mimed a complicated set of actions. His guards watched, looking puzzled. Finally he gave up. "In the Igor Recycling plant!" he exclaimed. "I'm a king, not a mime."

Igor's eyes widened in fear. The Igor Recycling plant! He struggled furiously, but his captors were far too strong. They carried him toward the chute in the wall.

"No! Please!" he cried, twisting against the iron grip of the guards.

Upstairs, Scamper and Brain had been watching unnoticed. Now they looked at each other in alarm as Igor came closer and closer to the chute.

"Eva, where are you?" Igor wailed as a guard reached forward to open the chute. And then with a heave-ho, Igor was tossed in, and the door clanged shut behind him. "EEEEVAAAAAAA!" Igor cried as he plummeted down the dark chute.

FOURTEEN

"Lock your doors and hide your loved ones. It's the fifty-first annual Evil Science Fair!" Carl Cristall sang out in front of the TV camera as Malaria prepared for its biggest night.

The turbulent weather provided the perfect backdrop for the yearly celebration of all things evil. From every direction, torch-wielding mobs of villagers moved toward the Killiseum, each group trailing the carriage of an Evil Scientist. Other Malarians were already inside the Killiseum, finding seats and buying T-shirts and popcorn.

Cristall was hosting the live broadcast, which would be shown all over the world. He was in a booth overlooking the arena, sitting at a desk, wearing nothing but glasses and headphones.

"I'm Carl Cristall," he said into the camera, "coming to

you live and invisible!" He glanced down into the Killiseum. "Fans are taking their seats, including King Malbert himself." He noticed that the king didn't look very happy as he sat down among his guards in the royal box. But he decided it might not be tactful—or safe—to say so. "Meanwhile," the host went on, "the Evil Scientists are in their locker rooms prepping their Evil Inventions."

Down by the locker rooms, Dr. Schadenfreude's carriage had just pulled in. The Evil Scientist helped Eva out.

"Here we are," he told her grandly, "a dressing room fit for a leading lady."

Eva looked thrilled. She was trying not to let Igor's betrayal ruin her big audition. After all, the show must go on; every true actress knew that.

"Wow," she exclaimed as a muffled cheer went up outside. "How many producers are on this project?"

"I'm going to go save him," Brain announced, peering down the Igor Recycling chute.

"Wait—," Scamper began.

"Look!" Brain cut him off. "Maybe I'm an idiot. But I know one thing—I have to try."

Scamper shook his head. "No," he said. "I was going to say, 'Wait, I'm coming with you.'"

Brain smiled. "On three," he said. "One, two . . ."

He shoved Scamper down the chute before finishing his count. "Hey!" Scamper shouted.

"Five!" Brain called out, before leaping into the dark tunnel.

The two of them tumbled down, head over paws and wheel over robotic arm. When they fell out at the other end, they were caught by a conveyer belt, which left them hanging upside down—right next to Igor!

Igor couldn't have been more surprised to see his two friends. "What are you doing here?" he cried.

"We're here to rescue you!" Brain announced proudly.

Igor's whole body drooped. "Well, I don't really want to be rescued," he said sadly. "I'm an Igor, and this is what happens to us."

"Figures," Scamper muttered. "Just when I decided I want to live!"

Dr. Schadenfreude checked his watch and tapped his foot impatiently. Eva was nothing but a gargantuan silhouette behind a screen as she put on her costume.

"Don't peek!" she called out playfully.

The Evil Scientist shuddered, but he did his best to keep the disgust out of his voice as he called back, "Don't worry!"

"I hope I can still do a decent audition without Igor's help," Eva said, sounding a bit worried.

"Trust me," Dr. Schadenfreude replied, glad that Eva was behind the screen so she couldn't see his sly smile. "I'm the one who's going to bring out the *real* you."

Igor, Scamper, and Brain were still hanging upside down, moving closer and closer to the Recycler. The huge machine thumped and whirred alarmingly. But Igor didn't seem to notice—or care.

"This isn't you, Igor," Scamper said. "Where's all that stupid optimism and that annoying can-do attitude?"

"I tried to be someone different," Igor said. "But the world wouldn't let me."

Brain took out Eva's necklace. He dangled it in front of Igor. "Don't you want to go after Eva and save her from Schadenfreude?" he asked.

"Are you actually trying to hypnotize me, Brain?" Igor asked.

"Yes," Brain said. "But if that's not working, then how about this?" He swung the necklace hard.

"Ow!" Igor yelped, grabbing his head.

"Eva needs you," Brain continued. "You're the only hunchback that can stand tall and fight for her!"

Igor blinked. Brain might be a complete moron, but this time he was right!

"Brain, that may be the smartest thing you've ever said." Igor glanced at the Recycler churning along just ahead. They needed a plan right now!

With renewed motivation, Igor figured out what they had to do. There was a button on the wall to one side of the conveyor belt. Brain's robotic arm was pretty long. If he could swing far enough in that direction, he might be able to hit the button and release them from the conveyor belt.

"Reach, Brain, reach!" he cried as Brain swung for it for the third or fourth time.

But once again, Brain came up a little short. "You should have built me with a longer arm," he grumbled.

Over and over Brain tried, but the button was just too far away. Finally he collapsed, exhausted. Igor desperately tried to come up with a new plan.

Suddenly Scamper stepped right next to the button. Brain and Igor both stared at him in shock. Huh?

Scamper shrugged. "What?" he said. "Like this is the first time I've gnawed off my own feet?"

Igor glanced at the conveyor belt. Scamper's feet were still dangling from it. He smiled as Scamper hit the button.

The conveyor belt let go, dropping Igor and Brain to the floor.

Igor rubbed his head and stood up. At that moment a siren blared and warning lights started flashing all through the Recycling plant, followed by shouts from outside.

"Oops," Scamper said. "Who says rabbits' feet are lucky?"

As the sirens wailed, the three of them burst out of the Recycling plant and found themselves in a shadowy tunnel lined with flickering torches. Workers from all over the plant had responded to the alarm, dropping whatever they were doing to give chase.

Igor and Scamper ran as fast as they could down the tunnel. Brain was falling behind as he paused to yank on each of the torches they were passing.

"What are you doing?" Scamper yelled.

"Looking for the secret passage!" Brain explained, panting. "There's always a secret passage."

They raced around a turn in the tunnel. Uh-oh! Another group of workers was coming toward them. Igor looked around. With workers chasing them on both ends, the only option seemed to be an opening just off the main tunnel nearby. He raced into it with his friends right behind him. But it turned out to be just a shallow alcove—a dead end.

Brain grabbed at the torch lighting the alcove. But once again, the wall stayed solid and unmoved.

"There's no secret passage, Brain." Igor collapsed wearily against the wall behind him, all the excitement of getting out and rescuing Eva quickly disappearing. "It's over."

Just then a stone moved under his hand. With a soft crunch, the wall slid back, revealing a circular staircase.

Brain smiled. "You were saying?"

Igor shrugged. "Technically, it's not a secret passage," he pointed out as they rushed in, the wall sliding closed behind them. "It's a secret *staircase*."

FIFTEEN

The staircase led up. And up. And then up some more. By the time Igor, Scamper, and Brain emerged at the top, they were all gasping for breath.

"Where . . . are . . . we?" Brain gasped. "And why am I panting? I don't have lungs."

They appeared to be in a huge, open room. They were so high up that the dark cloud cover that always hovered over Malaria surrounded them on all sides. Igor looked down and saw the packed Killiseum far below.

"The tower of the king's castle," he guessed. "Look, there's the Killiseum."

Brain pointed to the immense beam of light shooting up into the cloud cover. "That's the biggest flashlight I've ever seen," he commented.

"It's the Beacon of Evil," Scamper said, slightly

awestruck. "We are at the top of the Royal Castle."

The beacon was pouring out of a huge, dark machine. Igor stared at it. He'd seen it before on TV, of course, but this was his first time seeing it in person, and from this vantage point. He studied it, then looked curiously at the beam of light.

"Wait," he said. "*Is* it a beacon?"

Before his friends could answer, Igor spotted a ladder that was built into a wall. It went all the way up to the ceiling. He hurried over and started climbing.

"Where are you going?" Brain cried.

Igor barely heard him. With a determined look on his face, he climbed even faster.

King Malbert was not happy. But he was pretending to be his usual affable self as the cameras focused on him in the Royal Box.

"Welcome!" he called out jovially, speaking both to the cameras and to the throngs of Malarian citizens cheering below. "To you and the millions of viewers around the globe! They come from all corners . . ."

He paused at this point, just as he did every year. On the big screen in the middle of the arena, his face disappeared. Other pictures flashed up there—the faces of people from all over the world. Families, old people, little children of all races and creeds. The only thing they had in common was that they all looked petrified.

"And just look at them!" the king chuckled. He always got a kick out of this part. "They're all worried sick about one thing: world peace. Well tonight, it's within their grasp. It has but a small price, and that price is"—here he paused dramatically—"one hundred billion dollars!"

The crowd let out a collective *Ooooooh!*

The king smiled. "I, for one, think they can do it. Because if they don't, the last Evil Invention standing will be unleashed on the world and"—he shook his head sadly— "ugh. It's just too horrible to imagine."

At the top of the ladder, Igor found a hatch. He pushed it open, climbed through . . . and found himself in bright sunlight! He straightened up slowly, tipping his face upward. Warm, golden light bathed his skin. It was the first time in his life he'd ever stood in the sunlight.

It was the most beautiful thing he had ever seen.

Igor didn't let himself stop to enjoy it for long. Stepping to the edge of the tower, he looked down. The black cloud cover was now below him. And from up here, he could see clearly that the beam shooting up from the machine in the King's Tower was actually *creating* more black clouds. And they spread all around, creeping outward to cover the entire kingdom of Malaria with their darkness.

Igor heard the faint sound of the king's voice drifting up to him, carried by the loudspeakers inside the Killiseum. "So," the king was saying, "citizens of the world, call the number on the bottom of your screens. You *need* to give. Just like we in Malaria *need* to be evil."

Igor was stunned when he finally realized what he was seeing. "Malbert is making the clouds," he exclaimed. "He lied to us!"

All his life, he had believed in the king. He had believed that he was doing everything he could to make Malaria a better place. Now he knew that wasn't true.

But what was he going to do about it?

"How do I look?" Eva primped in front of the dressing-room mirror. Talk about opening-night jitters! She was a bundle of nerves.

And Dr. Schadenfreude wasn't helping much, gazing at her with his intense eyes. "The question is, how do you *feel*?" he asked.

Eva took a deep breath. "I feel . . . good," she said.

Dr. Schadenfreude shook his head. "Wrong answer."

"Huh?"

He took a step closer. "You need to feel evil."

"I know my choreography, if that's what you mean," Eva said, a little confused. Why did he have to talk in riddles so close to showtime?

"I think you need to go deeper," Dr. Schadenfreude urged. "Have you ever done anything evil?"

Eva didn't even have to think about her reply. "No," she said.

"Well, then, how can you play it truthfully? You can't get this part if you fake it."

Eva felt a twinge of concern. Was that true? She thought back over all her acting training.

"Hit me," Dr. Schadenfreude said.

"What?"

"Hit me," he repeated.

Eva was shocked. "I could never hit anyone!"

"My God!" Dr. Schadenfreude shook his head. "Igor was right. You're not an actress."

"Yes, I am," Eva retorted.

"No, you're not." The scientist sighed. "No wonder he chose Heidi. I mean, she's beautiful, you're not. She has talent, you do not."

Eva scowled and clenched her fists. "Don't say that!"

"Look at you." He waved one hand at her dismissively. "You're pathetic."

"No, I'm not!" Eva's blood was starting to boil now. How dare he?

"You're just a big, fat, ugly monster. And you couldn't act your way out of a—"

Smack! One massive hand swung at him, sending him flying across the room.

Eva gasped, shocked by what she'd done. Meanwhile, inside the tip of her finger, hidden by a layer of steely gray skin, her Evil Bone started to pulse and glow.

Her shock faded. Her eyes flashed, then went as dark and angry as the eternal night outside. Her face twisted into a cruel sneer.

Dr. Schadenfreude looked up from where he'd landed in a heap on the floor. Blood trickled from his nose, but he wiped it away, unfazed.

"We're ready," he said with a satisfied smile.

SIXTEEN

"Let's get evil!" Carl Cristall howled into the microphone.

The crowd screamed with anticipation. They stamped their feet, waved their arms, and whistled. In the Royal Box, the king watched it all without much interest. But he kept a careful eye on the cameras. Whenever they turned his way, he made sure to grin and wave as if he were having the time of his life.

Up in the Royal Tower, Igor heard the explosion of cheers that came from far below. He was down in the tower's main archway, holding on to a long chain connected to the top of the tower. He bent over and eyed the top of the Killiseum. Brain and Scamper were watching him.

"You're going to lower yourself down with that?" Brain asked.

111

Igor's voice held steely determination as he replied, "You've got your job. I've got mine." He stepped off the edge and started carefully lowering himself down. "I'm coming, Eva!" he cried.

He was so overcome at the very utterance of her name that he lost his grip. The chain flew out of his hand. He started to fall, but then his foot hit the chain and got caught in it. He was yanked to a halt, hanging upside down.

"Phew! That was . . . *Aiiiiiiiii!*"

The chain came loose at the top, and everything—chain, Igor, and all—went tumbling down, down, down . . .

WHOMP! Igor slammed down hard, face-first, onto the Killiseum roof. Slowly he pushed himself up, shaking his head to try to clear it.

"I'm . . . coming . . . Eva," he repeated.

Down on the floor of the Killiseum, the sounds of the crowd were deafening. Around the circular arena were thirteen giant doors. Above each door was a battle station, one for each of Malaria's thirteen Evil Scientists. But this year, only twelve stations were manned by an Evil Scientist and his Igor. Dr. Glickenstein's station was empty.

Baby-headed Dr. Kindermann was ready for action. He gave the signal to his Igor to pull a lever, which opened the door below them. The crowd let out an *Ooooh!* as a giant teddy bear marionette toddled out onto the Killiseum floor. It growled, much to everyone's delight.

One by one the other doors opened as well, releasing one horrible and destructive invention after another: a blob monster, a towering robot, an evil orb, a giant Venus flytrap . . . the Evil Science Fair was truly the ultimate celebration of everything wicked—and deadly.

As the defending champion, Dr. Schadenfreude was the last to present his creation. In his Royal Box the king leaned forward, looking nervous as the Evil Scientist gestured to his Igor.

"It's time for my 'crowning' achievement," Dr. Schadenfreude said with a smirk. His Igor pulled the lever, and the door slid open.

The crowd fell silent as Eva stepped out and straightened to her full height. Her huge wig shone under the arena lights. The same lights glinted off the shiny buttons on her dress and reflected off her polished shoes. But no light found its way out of her evil black eyes.

She took her position on the field of battle and glanced around at the competition. One person in the crowd finally found his voice.

"Ooh, look!" he cried. "It's an evil lady monster!"

A few people laughed, then a few more. Within seconds, the whole place was howling.

"It's a crime to have a face like that!" someone yelled out.

"She needs a bag to cover it!" someone else shouted.

The king grinned. He peered down at Dr. Schadenfreude, who looked annoyed.

Meanwhile Igor had just climbed down from the roof and into the upper section of the arena. He spotted Eva down on the ground far below.

"Eva!" he called out.

Just then she turned her head, still surveying the other inventions. Igor gasped as he caught a glimpse of her black eyes and cruel sneer.

"No!" he cried, his heart sinking, as the laughter and jeers grew louder. Then Eva stomped forward and sang. She was going to show everyone that she was a real actress.

With each word she sang, Eva began to strike. *SLAM!* She smashed the evil orb into a wall, where it crackled and fizzled out.

The crowd was momentarily stunned by the sudden, deadly move. A hush fell over the Killiseum. Then the place erupted in cheers.

Dr. Schadenfreude smiled. He shot one more glance at Eva as she stomped toward her next opponent. Then he stepped out of his battle station. He had other business to take care of now.

The cheers grew louder and louder as Eva demolished one Evil Invention after another.

SPLURT! She crushed the blob monster.

SKZZZT! She ripped the head off the robot.

Meanwhile, Igor was struggling to push his way down through the crowd. "Let me through!" he cried. "I made her!"

"You made her?" a big guy in the crowd laughed, then grabbed Igor by the collar, hoisting him right off his feet. "Hey, everyone, here's the genius *Igor* that made her!"

Everyone shouted with laughter. Some of them grabbed Igor and tossed him around in an impromptu mosh pit. Igor struggled to get away.

"Wait, no!" he cried desperately. "Eva!"

Down in the arena, Eva was still singing and smashing. When the giant Venus flytrap attacked her, she grabbed it by the vines. Swinging it around and around over her head, she wound up and let go, hurling it right out of the stadium. The crowd went wild.

Up in the Royal Box, King Malbert had sunk down in

115

his seat. After that first glorious moment when it seemed that Dr. Schadenfreude's invention was simply a joke, he had sunk back into a depression. "I can't believe he did it again," he muttered.

Suddenly Dr. Schadenfreude strolled into the box with Jaclyn at his side. The king frowned. "What are you doing up here, Shoddy?" he demanded.

"I was about to ask you the same question, *Malby*," Dr. Schadenfreude responded, flashing a wicked smile.

"*Malby?*" The king drew himself up to his full, regal height. "What is the meaning of this?"

"This means you're through," Dr. Schadenfreude declared as he snatched the crown off King Malbert's head. "Or, should I say, this means you're *overthrown*."

Before the king could respond, the Evil Scientist grabbed him and tossed him over the edge of the box into the arena below. King Malbert scrambled to his feet, looking around in terror at the Evil Inventions around him. Then he ran for his life.

Up in the box, the Royal Guards were quick to seize Dr. Schadenfreude. But Jaclyn stepped forward.

"Unhand him," she ordered. "He's your new king."

Dr. Schadenfreude smirked. "And if you have a problem with that," he added, "please take it up with

116

the head of my complaints department."

He pointed to Eva. At that moment, she was ripping the head off an animal-shaped robot, singing at the top of her lungs all the while. The guards let go of Dr. Schadenfreude immediately.

In the Royal Tower, Scamper and Brain were busy trying to pull apart the control panel of the machine that controlled the Beacon of Evil. It wasn't easy as the entire narrow tower was rocking back and forth with each stomp of Eva's tremendous feet.

Brain was listening to the monstrous singing with growing panic. "She's almost at her big finish," he said, his voice shaking.

Scamper nodded grimly. "And when that fat lady sings, it's *really* over."

SEVENTEEN

"*Today! Today!*" Eva bellowed. She smashed another Evil Invention and looked around.

She blinked her huge, evil black eyes. That had been the last of them. Springs, coils, weapons, and robotic body parts lay scattered across the arena floor in a horrific path of destruction.

The crowd was going crazy, already chanting their approval of the new champion. But Eva wasn't finished with her song yet.

Igor had finally escaped from the mosh pit and rushed the rest of the way down through the bleachers. Now he looked down at the arena. Eva was looking around as she sang, deciding on her next move. Igor's whole body went cold as he realized he knew what it was.

"She's going to take this whole place apart!" he cried.

Eva had just found the thick support columns that held the entire stadium together. Huge cables protruded from the columns, and with a mighty yank, Eva tore the cables from the columns. Parts of the Killiseum started to shake, and when Eva pulled again, the entire arena rumbled alarmingly.

Eva sang on, yanking away. She was close to her big finish. As huge chunks of the roof and walls fell into the crowd, their cheers quickly turned into screams of terror.

Eva let go of the cables. She took a deep breath and started to spin. It was time for her finale, the special move she had been practicing back in Glickenstein's castle. That time she had taken out only that one support column in the lab. But this time . . .

"Wait!" A single voice cut through the clamor of the shrieking, sobbing crowd.

Eva paused in midspin. She recognized that voice. Turning, she saw a small figure standing alone amid the wreckage of the arena floor. It was Igor.

"Eva," he called pleadingly. "This isn't you."

Eva blinked, trying to focus on the tiny figure through the thick cloud of evil that had taken over her mind. What was it saying?

"I *did* create you to be evil," Igor continued, "and I'm sorry I lied to you. I lied to you about everything. But this is just a role and you don't have to play it."

The fog in Eva's mind lifted a little. Now she felt confused.

"Yes, you do!" another voice commanded. It was Dr. Schadenfreude, calling down to her from the Royal Box. "He's an Igor, and you're an Evil Invention. You're *evil!*"

Igor ignored him, still speaking directly to Eva. "No," he said. "Everyone has an Evil Bone in their body, but we choose whether or not to use it. And as someone I love once said, 'It's better to be a good nobody than an evil somebody.'"

Eva blinked again. Igor watched her carefully. Were his words getting through to her? Or was it too late?

Then as he stared up at her, he noticed the sky lightening overhead. The clouds were starting to clear over the Killiseum—and all over Malaria! Brain and Scamper had come through after all. They were able to turn off the Beacon of Evil.

Eva noticed the change in the sky as well. She looked up, squinting against the increasing brightness.

One sunbeam cut through the haze, then another. There were gasps of awe and amazement from the

120

crowd as the sunlight poured down, brighter and brighter.

Eva stared up into the light for a long moment. The warmth of the sun felt strange, but nice. Light touched her face, her arms, her fingers—and deactivated her Evil Bone.

When Eva finally looked down at Igor, her eyes weren't black anymore. They were filled with tears. "I'm not evil," she said softly. "I'm Eva."

Igor's heart flooded with gladness as bright as the sky overhead. The real Eva was back!

"Igor, I felt like I was in a dark, horrible place," Eva admitted.

Igor nodded. He knew exactly how she felt. "We all were."

At that moment King Malbert crawled out from beneath a twisted scrap of metal on the field. He stared upward in horror.

"Wait!" he cried. "What's happening?"

"The end of Malaria's evil role in the world," Igor answered. Just then he noticed his own face up on the JumboTron. His next words poured out of the loudspeakers. "For generations, King Malbert has kept us in the dark by *creating* the clouds with a weather ray!" he announced.

The crowd murmured in shock as Igor continued. "He lied to us. We trusted him and he lied to us. He tricked us into thinking we needed to be evil to survive. But we don't. None of us do."

"This is outrageous!" the king cried. He jabbed one finger at Igor. "He has no proof. Where's his proof? I demand to see proof!"

SPLAT! At that moment the weather machine tumbled down from the Tower. It landed right on King Malbert, squashing him.

"Oops," Brain said, peering down from the Tower window.

In every part of the stadium, the citizens of Malaria were abuzz about all that had just happened. Until then, Dr. Schadenfreude had been watching the proceedings from the Royal Box. Now sensing that things were spinning out of his control, the Evil Scientist wildly waved his arms to get everyone's attention.

"King Malbert the liar is dead!" he shouted. "Long live King Schadenfreude! Long live King Schaden—"

SMASH! Eva swung her arm, knocking the Royal Box off its perch. Dr. Schadenfreude and Jaclyn tumbled out, landing in the dirt of the arena floor.

"That's my last evil act," Eva declared. "From here on

122

out, all evil doings will be handled by my manager-slash-boyfriend."

Igor smiled as Eva picked Dr. Schadenfreude up by the collar. His legs swung helplessly, and he waved his fist.

"I command you to put me down!" he cried. "I'm the king of Malaria!"

The crowd booed. Jaclyn stood up and brushed herself off.

"Well, that was a short reign," she noted. "Hey, fellas! I'm single again!"

"Don't worry," Igor told Dr. Schadenfreude. "We have another job for you, Shoddy. One you were born to do."

EPILOGUE

A few months later, Malaria was a different place. The sun rose over it every day, just like it did over the rest of the world. The plants came back. Birds started singing in the trees. People remembered how to be good instead of evil.

The Killiseum had changed too. Now it was an amphitheater. The marquee outside read, MALARIA COMMUNITY THEATER. Inside, a man dressed as a giant pickle wandered through the crowd carrying a tray with a sign that read, POEKELMACHER'S PICKLES: THEY'RE WICKED GOOD!

"Pickles," Dr. Schadenfreude—for it was him, of course—called out without enthusiasm. "Get your gherkins here."

Nearby, Carl Cristall stepped forward with a microphone as a familiar hunchbacked figure hurried into the theater. Cristall's cameraman lifted his camera.

124

"President Igor!" Cristall shouted. "Isn't it true that you brought back the sun to punish invisible naturalists who will now be victims of sunburn?"

"What? No," Igor told the TV personality. "And you can't get sunburned, Carl. Light passes through you."

He hurried off. Cristall stared blankly into the camera before exclaiming, "The man's a genius! That's why we elected him!"

Igor was already on his way backstage. When he got there, he saw Scamper adjusting the costumes on some of the blind orphans who were in that day's production.

"Scamper," he called. "Have you seen Eva?"

"No. Go away," Scamper replied, annoyed at being interrupted. He reached for one of the kids' costumes. "Hans, you're wearing this backward!" he snapped. "What are you, blin—" He caught himself. "I mean, let's, uh, switch this around."

Igor hurried on, passing Brain, who was dressed in a tuxedo and talking to a pretty girl.

"So what do you do?" the girl asked Brain.

"This," Brain said proudly, making his wheel squeak.

Igor finally spotted Eva. "Sorry I'm late!" he said. "I left your opening-night gift back at the lab."

He held his hand out toward Eva. Dangling from it was

a familiar chain with a silver canister attached.

"My necklace!" Eva cried with delight.

"Look inside."

She opened it up and pulled out a scroll of paper. When she unrolled it, her eyes went wide.

"Oh my gosh!" she cried. "You're really going to make this?"

"Yeah," Igor said, shrugging. "But if it doesn't work, then we'll just adopt."

They both glanced down at Igor's plans, which were blueprints for a gigantic, patched-together dog.

"It's a big step, getting a pet together," Eva mused.

Igor grinned. "Come on, after living with Brain and Scamper, everything will seem like a breeze."

But there was no more time for discussion. It was showtime!

Igor and Eva stood together and watched the curtain rise, Igor's heart swelling as the choir of orphans began to sing. Overhead, the sun beamed down on the theater. Eva crouched down to rest her head on Igor's shoulder.

It was a bright, beautiful day in Malaria. And it would stay that way—always. Igor was sure of that.